SHADOWS OF THE PAST

A DI KAREN HEATH CRIME NOVEL

JAY NADAL

Published by 282publishing.com

Copyright @ Jay Nadal 2024

All rights reserved.

Jay Nadal has asserted his right to be identified as the author of this work.

No part of this book may be reproduced, stored in any retrieval system, or transmitted in any form or by any means, electronic, mechanical, photocopying, recording or otherwise, without the prior written permission of the author.

This book is a work of fiction, names, characters, businesses, organizations, places and events other than those clearly in the public domain, are either the product of the author's imagination or used fictitiously. Any resemblance to actual persons, living or dead, events or locales is entirely coincidental.

PROLOGUE

The musty odour of dampness and decay assaulted the man's nostrils, the pungent stench permeating every corner of the dark, cavernous space. His eyelids felt heavy, as if weighed down by an invisible force, but he forced them open, blinking to adjust to the pitch-black void that surrounded him. A throbbing ache pounded in his head, the remnants of blows that had rendered him briefly unconscious, leaving him disoriented and confused.

He struggled against the restraints, yanking against them as he tried in vain to move his arms. They were bound behind the rigid back of the chair, with the cable ties digging into his wrists. The plastic cut into his skin, leaving angry red marks and sending sharp jolts of pain up his arms with every futile attempt to break free. Though his legs were not restrained, he felt too feeble to wriggle free, as his muscles were weak and unresponsive. A lack of food and water had drained him of all energy, leaving him a mere shell of his former self.

As the damp chill crept into his bones, a tremor rocked his body, causing him to shiver uncontrollably in discomfort while his thin T-shirt and tatty jumper provided no warmth or protection against the unforgiving cold. The fabric clung to his skin, damp with perspiration and the condensation that hung heavy in the air. Little met his blurred gaze, just dark walls and ground with the odd small light scattered round him, their feeble glow doing little to help him make sense of his surroundings.

He strained his eyes, desperate to make sense of these stark surroundings and how he'd found himself here, searching for any clue that might shed light on his predicament. Nothing. No clue to his whereabouts or fate. But the darkness was absolute, suffocating, pressing in on him from all sides like a physical force. He opened his mouth to scream, but the words caught in his parched throat, his vocal cords constricted by fear and dehydration, so they came out as nothing more than a rattle, a pitiful sound.

Time alone marked his agony, each second a silent sentinel in the endless dark. The deafening silence bore down on him, broken only by the sound of his own laboured breathing and the pounding of his heart in his ears. Ragged breaths escaped his cracked, parched lips as white plumes that hung in the frigid air before melting away, a fleeting reminder of his own fragile mortality.

"Please, help me. Why am I here?" he pleaded, his voice a hoarse whisper that echoed weakly. His teeth chattered as tremors coursed through his body, his muscles spasming to generate warmth. Though he looked round, nothing moved. Was he here alone? Had they left him here to die alone, abandoned, and forgotten?

His mind tracked back to the men. Dangerous men. Their faces shadowed and indistinct in his memory. They'd offered him fifty quid and a warm bed if he came with them, a tempting proposition for someone who'd been living rough for so long. There was a lot he could do with fifty quid. That would buy him a lot of gear, and perhaps a hot soup and sandwich to fill his empty belly. But it was the drugs that fuelled his body, the only thing that kept him going, helping him cope with life on the streets. A place where no one cared, where shoppers would turn the other way when he asked for spare change, and where his bed was a sheet of cardboard and a grubby sleeping bag, scavenged from the rubbish and reeking of other people's misery.

He coughed, the violent spasms rattling his ribcage, each intake of air a frosty shard of glass slicing at his raw throat and lungs. The pain was excruciating, but he couldn't stop, his body convulsing with each hacking cough. Momentary clouds ballooned from his mouth with every strained exhalation, only to be consumed by the oppressive blackness surrounding him like a hungry void, eager to devour any sign of life.

His head snapped up, and his heart pounded as a scuffing sound tore him from his thoughts, yanking him back to the nightmarish reality of his situation. At first, he noticed only subtle movements in the pitch-blackness—flickers of motion at the edges of his vision, resembling ghostly apparitions dancing beyond the reach of his perception. Then, they materialised from the void like ethereal spectres as more than a dozen figures took shape, their forms coming together out of the darkness.

His eyes strained to make them out, to bring them into focus, but the gloom was too thick, too impenetrable. Were they ghosts or nightmarish hallucinations conjured up by his weary mind, fractured by fear and desperation? No... as more details sluggishly came into focus, he realised with a sinking feeling that they were men, at least a dozen hulking silhouettes emerging from the subterranean murk, their faces obscured by shadows.

A guttural sound of primal terror escaped his constricted throat, a strangled cry that was part whimper, part scream. Had they been there all along, watching his anguish and desperation from the shroud of darkness? Observing his pitiful gasps for life like carrion crows lying in wait, ready to pick his bones clean? Icy tendrils of dread tore through his core at the realisation that this nightmare was only just beginning, that he was at their mercy, a plaything for their twisted amusement.

He closed his eyes, hot tears streaming down his face as he silently prayed for a swift end, for the blessed release of oblivion. But deep down, he knew that his prayers would go unanswered, that these faceless tormentors were doomed to make him suffer, and that his screams would echo unheard in the void.

1

ONLY SIX WEEKS ago Karen and Jade were at the North Middlesex University Hospital, dread etched on their faces as they made their way to Steve's room. Both had received the devastating news that their former colleague, Steve Nugent, had been involved in a horrific accident which had left him with life-threatening injuries. During her first visit, though she was visibly shaken from seeing the extent of his injuries, Karen had prayed that it wouldn't be the last time she saw him. Six weeks later, he was still battling for his life.

Most of the life-support equipment had been removed and Steve remained in a stable but precarious condition. Several surgeries later, and many of his broken bones pinned together, he was conscious though plagued by searing pain. Karen and Jade sat on either side of his bed, fussing over him like two concerned mothers tending to their poorly child.

"I really appreciate you guys coming to see me," Steve said, his voice soft and strained. Still dosed up on powerful painkillers, he drifted in and out of moments of lucidity, his eyelids growing heavy.

"Don't be daft," Karen said. "You can't keep us away. I'm sorry we are so far away otherwise you would have the pleasure of our company most days." She gave him a warm smile, hoping to raise his spirits.

"I don't know if that's a good or bad thing," he replied, the hint of a grin playing across his pale features.

"Well, if we'd been here most days, we would have cramped your style and blown your chances with most of the nurses here." She glanced at Jade and winked.

Steve managed a faint smile at Karen's teasing. "I don't think Metal Mickey is up to much these days."

They sat in silence for a few moments, just enjoying each other's company. Being in hospital could be a lonely, soul-destroying time and so many patients always looked forward to visits from friends and family to cheer up their day. If Karen was being honest, being here was cheering up her day as well. She'd been through thick and thin with Steve, shared both joyous celebrations and heart-wrenching tragedies. She couldn't stand the thought of losing him as a friend. She knew Steve was a damn good officer, dedicated and professional, and she was certain he would be itching to get back to work as soon as possible.

"Any idea how long they'll keep you here for?" Jade asked, her warm brown eyes filled with concern.

Steve let out a weary sigh and shrugged a shoulder. "Optimistically, I would like to say weeks, but I think it could be a few months. I haven't been out of bed yet, so the physios don't know how easy or difficult it will be for me to regain my mobility and walk again. It's going to be an uphill battle for sure."

Karen reached out and gave Steve's hand a reassuring squeeze. "You're a fighter, Steve. You've got through the worst of it. The doctors are hopeful that you will make a full recovery, even if it takes time."

"Yeah, and because of that, Karen and I were arguing as to who could get your car!" Jade laughed, trying to inject some much-needed humour into the sombre atmosphere.

Karen rolled her eyes good-naturedly at her friend's jest. "Don't listen to her, she is hilarious today. Not."

"Neither of you. It's a bloke's car. Brad would get it," Steve replied with mock indignation.

Karen and Jade both pulled faces of exaggerated disgust. "Sexist pig," Jade teased.

They continued catching up about life in London and how different it was to things back in York. Steve listened with interest, grateful for the distraction, but as time wore on Karen noticed his eyes start to droop and he became less interactive, the drugs pulling him under into a healing sleep.

"Hey, listen, you need to get some rest," Karen said softly. "We'll come back as soon as we can. In the meantime, if there's anything you need, send me a text. Get Brad to call me." She rose from her chair and leaned across the bed to gently kiss Steve's forehead in a sisterly gesture. Jade followed suit, placing a tender kiss on his brow. Steve offered a weak smile as his eyes slid closed once more. The two women made their way to the door, looking back once to their sleeping friend before reluctantly heading off.

"He looks a lot better than the last time," Karen remarked as they waited for the lift, relieved to see some of the colour returning to Steve's face.

Jade nodded in agreement. "The bruising on his face is going down at least."

The silvery doors slid back with a soft chime. They

stepped in and Karen pressed the button for the ground floor. "What time are you meeting Wainwright?" Jade asked.

Karen checked the time on her phone. It wouldn't be long until she saw Wainwright again, the pathologist in London that she'd struck up a strong bond and friendship with while based the Met. "An hour. He's booked us a table for dinner in Shoreditch. An Indian restaurant, apparently."

Jade's brow furrowed in confusion. "I thought Wainwright didn't like Indian food? Said it was too spicy for his delicate palate or some bollocks like that?"

"That's what I thought too," Karen said with a shrug. "Maybe he's stopped being such a baby and decided to broaden his culinary horizons." The lift chimed again, and the doors opened. They headed for the exit, the cacophony of sounds and harsh artificial lighting a jarring contrast to the quiet peace of Steve's room.

"Shall I call you at nine and we can decide where to meet up before we head back?" Karen asked as they emerged on to the busy street.

"Yep, sounds good. I'm meeting Sophia and Grace for a few drinks in Leicester Square first. So it won't be a late one," Jade confirmed.

They both headed off in different directions. Karen jumped into her car while Jade made her way towards the nearest Tube station. Though their hearts were still heavy with worry for their friend, they took comfort in seeing Steve making progress, his indomitable spirit shining through. They knew he had a long road of recovery ahead, but Steve was a fighter—he would get through this too, with their love and support buoying him every step of the way.

2

Shoreditch was a vibrant, trendy neighbourhood in East London, renowned for its edgy, artistic vibe. Once a run-down area synonymous with the seedy underbelly of the city, it had undergone a renaissance in recent decades, transforming it into one of London's hippest hang-outs.

The streets formed a labyrinth of converted warehouse buildings with exposed brickwork, hip cafés, walls covered in street art, and cool bars and nightclubs. Graffiti murals and urban art installations adorned nearly every surface, giving the entire area the impression of an open-air gallery. It exuded a raw, creative energy that drew in artists, musicians, and the ultra-trendy crowd like a magnet.

At night, that energy level kicked up several notches as Shoreditch's bouncing clubs, underground raves, and secret speakeasies came alive. Edgy fashionistas, hipsters, musicians, and artists spilled out on to the streets, filling the bars and cafés until the early hours. The air hummed with an intoxicating blend of thumping bass lines, clinking glasses, and raucous laughter.

It was one of the many reasons Karen loved Shoreditch. She'd worked this patch many times over the years and had seen the worst the area offered—crime, poverty, a violent underworld festering beneath the glossy veneer. And yet, everyone wanted to hang out here because the vibrancy and ultra-cool atmosphere seamlessly interwove with those darker essences. A delicious dichotomy that added to Shoreditch's allure.

Karen followed the directions Wainwright had given her, the streets growing more crowded the deeper into the heart of Shoreditch she went. It didn't take long for her to notice him loitering outside the restaurant, looking clearly out of place among the hipster crowds in his smart suit and tie.

"Wainwright!" she called out with a grin as she approached.

Wainwright wasn't one for displays of emotion, always straight down the line and strait-laced, but with a heart of gold underneath that proper exterior. He offered her a small, stiff smile as she drew near.

"Er... yes... it's good to see you," he replied, giving a little cough to clear his throat. "It's been a while. Shall we... go in?"

Karen nodded and Wainwright held the door open for her in that old-fashioned, gentlemanly way of his. The rich, spicy aroma of Indian food wrapped itself round her as she entered the lively restaurant. The space was already pretty full, with conversations and laughter buzzing all round as they were shown to their table tucked discreetly in the back corner. Ever the gentleman, Wainwright pulled out Karen's chair for her and pushed it in once she was seated, and then took his own seat opposite her.

He ordered drinks—a beer for both of them after Karen had persuaded him to have one too, rather than his usual glass of red wine. It felt like no time at all since they had last spent time together, their camaraderie and easy rapport slotting back into that familiar groove their friendship had forged over the years. There was no awkwardness or uncomfortable silences between them, just that effortless easiness with no airs and graces required. Wainwright was his usual prim and proper self, peppering their conversation with those dry flashes of sardonic humour that Karen loved so much. She, on the other hand, couldn't stop talking, so many stories and snippets of gossip from her new life in York tumbling forth in an enthusiastic torrent.

Before long, the food arrived and Karen's eyes widened with delight as the waiter laid out the succulent dishes before them. The rich, spicy aromas were completely intoxicating—warm and heady like the sweltering Indian heat itself. Indian cuisine had a knack for transporting you to those far-flung corners of the Indian continent where food was such an integral part of life, love, and friendship. A way to bring people together, sharing good food and better company.

Karen glanced across at Wainwright as he eyed the array of dishes. A spoon grasped in one hand and a torn chunk of fresh naan bread in the other. He appeared hesitant.

"I thought you didn't like Indian food?" she queried with a bemused smile.

Wainwright cleared his throat again in that awkward way of his. He always seemed to revert to that little throat-clearing tic during moments of discomfort. "I don't. It's not my favourite. Put it that way," he admitted. "But I chose it because I knew how much you loved Indian food."

Karen's face softened as she set down her beer bottle,

her heart swelling with affection for this sweet, thoughtful man. "Aw, Wainwright. You did all this for me?"

He pursed his lips and gave a single nod, the tips of his ears flushing pink with embarrassment.

"That's so sweet of you," she said, truly touched. "I really appreciate the gesture. But I would have been as happy with a pizza, or Chinese food... heck, even a bloody Subway sandwich would have been lovely. You didn't have to go to all this trouble for me."

"Well, I saw this as a bit of a celebration," Wainwright replied, spooning some creamy butter chicken on to his plate along with a mound of fragrant basmati rice. "You being back in London and all. And that... that pleases me more than anything else."

Karen sensed her eyes becoming misty at his earnest words, the sentiment behind them apparent. Not for the first time, she marvelled at what a good man Wainwright was. Hidden beneath his reserved exterior was a heart overflowing with kindness and compassion. She did care for him a great deal. He had been the one person she'd truly opened up to before meeting Zac, always listening without judgement and offering wise counsel when needed. Qualities that were so very rare to find in most men these days.

"Does it feel strange being back?" Wainwright asked after they started to eat.

Karen swallowed her mouthful and considered his question for a moment. "Yes and no, I suppose," she replied. "It feels familiar, which I love. So easy to just become another anonymous face in the crowd. London is lively and bustling, but the job of being a copper here is exhausting and mentally challenging, day in, day out. If I'd stayed in the Met, I'm not sure how much longer I could have stuck it out before the stress and grind of it all overwhelmed me. Don't get me wrong," she was quick to add, "I adore my job and I'm good at what I do. But I paid a high price for that career and so do many other officers. The toll it takes is immense."

Wainwright gave a sombre nod of understanding, having been there himself for many gruelling years on the front line. "And York?" he prompted. "How does that compare?"

"Like chalk and cheese," Karen said with a smile. "Laid-back, mostly. You experience a sense of belonging and connection to the locals in a way that's impossible in a large, anonymous city like London. And you'd never believe it, but I love the history and heritage of York, let alone the stunning surrounding countryside. It's beautiful, Wainwright. You have to find the time to come up and visit me one day—I'll show you all the best spots and sights. Who knows," she teased, "you might enjoy a change of scenery now and then."

"Perhaps I shall take you up on that offer," he agreed, allowing the faintest of smiles to crease the corners of his eyes. "I confess, I would quite like to see this city that lured you away from me... from us," he corrected, almost stumbling over the words.

Those last few words landed like a weighty blow as Karen put down her fork. "Oh, Wainwright..." she murmured, reaching across the table to give his hand a gentle squeeze. "You know I'm only a phone call away, don't you? Work keeps me anchored in York for now, but that doesn't make you any less important to me. I wish I could come down to see you more often. I miss our chats. But so much of my life is up there now."

She saw the disappointment flicker across Wainwright's features as he bowed his head to stare at his plate of food. "Besides," Karen continued in a lighter tone, trying to raise his spirits, "you'd probably be sick of me before too long. There's only so much of my moaning and groaning you can tolerate, eh?"

"It would be worth it," he murmured, his voice barely audible. Then, a little louder: "My biscuit tin feels quite abandoned without your... contributions."

Karen let out a hearty laugh at that, the tension broken as quickly as it had arisen. Trust Wainwright to cling to the habit that had irked him for so many years as his reason for missing her. They continued with their meal, the conversation flowing as it always did between them, Karen regaling him with amusing anecdotes from her new rural life until their plates were clean.

All too soon, it was time to leave the cosy warmth of the restaurant and brave the chill winter evening air once more. As they emerged on to the bustling street, Karen pulled Wainwright into a warm embrace.

"Thank you for the meal and the lovely catch-up," she said as they parted. "I enjoyed myself tonight."

Wainwright gave one of his small, self-conscious nods. "My pleasure. It was... worth it, to see you again. Let's not leave it so long next time, hmm?"

"I promise." Karen leaned in to plant a soft kiss on his cheek.

As she pulled back, she caught the bemused stares from a cluster of hipsters lounging nearby. Karen grinned and gave Wainwright's arm an affectionate squeeze.

"Safe journey home, Karen," he said, unable to quite meet her gaze as a blush crept up his neck.

With a last wave, Karen headed off towards where she had parked her car, a warm, comforting glow within. Seeing Wainwright again had felt just like old times—natural and so very right, like reuniting with the missing piece of a jigsaw puzzle she hadn't even realised was incomplete. She loved her new life in York, but moments like this made her realise just how much she had missed an integral part of her old existence, too. Vowing not to let so much time elapse before their next meeting, Karen slipped into her car with a contented smile, already looking forward to their next catch-up.

3

KAREN PARKED in the station car park and switched off the ignition. She yawned and rubbed her tired eyes. The journey back to York last night was easy enough, but the day had been long, draining, but fun too. It felt strange being back as she stared round the car park, the surrounding grounds, and the bony trees that reminded her of the bitterness of deep winter. She couldn't wait for spring and summer to return. If there was one thing she liked about the station, it was the grounds that they were set in.

Her mind drifted back to the summer when the smell of cut grass would waft in through her office window. She'd rise from her chair and watch the gardeners walk up and down the grass, the rumble of a petrol-driven mower drowning out the sounds of the birds in the trees.

She loved the openness and never thought in a million years that she would feel the freedom of space. London was tight, cramped, and oppressive. You couldn't turn in any direction without bumping into someone. York was different. Though her job was challenging, she had never felt so relaxed in her role as when she'd started here.

Karen grabbed her bag and keys and exited her car, locking it behind her. She hurried into her building, the biting chill of winter's wind slapping her in the face and cutting through her clothes. Though she had three layers on, she shivered. The second she stepped through the doors, a wall of heat bathed her face and prickled her skin. She said hello to officers as she passed them in the corridor before making a way up to the SCU and towards her office. The first thing she did was fire up her computer before she set about hanging up her coat and unpacking her laptop from her bag. While her computer sprung into life, Karen grabbed her mug and grimaced as she saw the brown sticky sludge of coffee stuck to the bottom. She'd forgotten to wash it.

Peeking through the glass wall to the main floor, Karen noticed officers were thin on the ground. A few of them were still on annual leave and would return in the next day or so. January was often a quieter month of the year. Most of the drama had happened towards the end of December with a rise in domestic assaults around Christmas, but thankfully no murders. Fights, stabbings, and general antisocial behaviour were the order of the day for most of her colleagues as they dealt with a rise in cases during December where a deadly mix of too much alcohol, parties, and drugs led to a spike in calls to the police.

She flicked on the kettle and waited for it to boil, spooning a large teaspoon of coffee granules into her cup. She poured the water into her mug but had to replace it hastily on its stand when her mobile rang. It was her boss.

"Morning, ma'am."

"Ah, good that you're in. I wasn't sure as I'd called through to your office and you didn't answer."

"Sorry, ma'am. I was rustling up a coffee."

"Okay, can you pop to my office quickly? Nothing major. Just a quick chat."

Karen let out a long, silent breath. "Of course, ma'am. I'll be there in a sec." Karen hung up and finished making her coffee before heading to Kelly's office. Kelly's door was open as Karen appeared in the doorway. She knocked to get her boss's attention.

"Come in. I wanted to catch you before you got on with the day's work. How was your visit to see Steve yesterday?"

"Very good. Thanks for asking, ma'am. Steve is recovering well, and he appears more upbeat. He's in for a long slog and reckons he'll be there for a few months. He hasn't been out of bed yet to see how well he can walk."

Kelly nodded and grimaced. "Not easy. Tough for any officer to deal with. But I'm glad he has you both, and I'm sure he appreciated the visit."

"My team really liked him, and even though I'm not there any more, I think it's important for us to show our support and let him know that we're thinking of him."

"Of course. Well, keep me updated on how he gets on. Also, during our last management meeting, we decided that we have the budget to push on with appointing a permanent DI on your team."

Karen raised a brow, shocked at the news. Kelly had been adamant for months that there was no wiggle room and that budgets were tight. She wondered why there had been a change. "Great, that's really good news."

"Yes, exciting. We'll begin screening candidates and setting up interviews in the coming weeks." Kelly paused for a moment and chewed on her bottom lip as she swivelled a pen on her desk. "I know you've been keen for Jade to be considered as your DI. Do you consider her to be ready for it?"

"I think so."

"Think so?"

"I know so, ma'am. It's why I asked her to join me in York. She is competent, capable, has fantastic people skills, and has the potential to go much further. The opportunities weren't there in London. Posts didn't come up that often, and inevitably, you were up against a lot of candidates."

"How well does she cope under stress?"

That was a tricky one in Karen's opinion. Jade displayed some hesitancy when stressed, but she was certain that was more down to a lack of experience of being placed in those situations. Stronger coping mechanisms would come with time and experience. But she wasn't about to tell Kelly that.

"In my opinion, she handles the situations well. I would be more than happy to let her take charge as the acting SIO on any investigation and be assured that she would handle it professionally."

"Who in your team would be a suitable candidate to replace Jade if she gets promoted?"

Karen nodded. "Belinda. She's shown me without any doubt that she is more than competent and capable. She's an incredible officer. Ed isn't that far behind, but he needs more experience. If we promote Belinda, it would provide Ed with the opportunity to further stretch himself."

"Okay, that's food for thought. We have two other internal candidates who we expect will apply for the DI role. And I've been informed that one external candidate from North Hants Police is looking to move to the area for family reasons. She is an acting DI already."

Shit. That wasn't good news.

"Right, keep this under wraps for now. Don't tell Jade, and as soon as we have firmed up the application process, you and I can have a word with her. You will be involved in reviewing applicants' details and the interview process, the first part of which will involve a panel interview. How does that sound?"

Karen smiled. "That sounds fair."

"Right, I'll get back to you soon as I know any more."

Karen thanked Kelly for her time before she headed back to the SCU. This was exciting but terrifying too. Karen had promised Jade that there was more opportunity for promotion in York than London, and she had hinted at the fact that she wanted Jade as her DI. What would happen if they overlooked Jade for promotion? The consequences were not worth considering.

Karen slipped through the doors to the main floor and took a seat at one of the spare desks. She sipped on her coffee as she watched her team and Jade. She was confident that Jade was ready, and she prayed that the promotion board would go her way. The interview process for the role of the DI was hard and challenging. The panel interview would throw various scenarios at her and assess how she would deal with them. Being put on the spot like that was extremely stressful and left little margin for error. There would also be an in-tray exercise where she would have to prioritise cases based on her review and then present her prioritising decisions to the panel. Karen shuddered at the thought.

She was proud of her team and enjoyed listening to the banter between them. Ed and Belinda impressed her a lot. They had become valuable assets to working as a cohesive unit. It was always scary starting up a new team. You never quite knew how team members would gel. Thankfully, it had benefited her. Ty had been an initial concern for her. A cheeky chappie, but took things a little too far, and wasn't as conscientious towards his work. But, in recent months he had *straightened out* and worked harder. Preet, Ned, and Claire were fantastic additions to her team. She leaned back in her chair, a smile plastered across her face. She loved working here.

4

KAREN'S MOMENT of quiet contemplation was short-lived when a call came through of a suspicious death. With Jade booked out for afternoon training, she asked Belinda to go with her. Tang Hall wasn't an area Karen was familiar with, but as they made their way in Karen's car to the location, it was interesting to hear Belinda's accounts of what the locals thought. One of the poorest areas of York, and close to the university, it had a mix of social housing, private rented accommodation for students, as well as normal hard-working families.

"It's not that bad, is it?" Karen asked as she slowed for the traffic ahead of her.

"It's not terrible. You won't find burnt-out cars all over the place. It's just a little scruffy. You're not going to get knifed or mugged, but there is a high incidence of drug-related offences in the area."

"What do we know about the victim?" Karen asked. Her satnav took her towards Carter Avenue, close to the community centre.

"Beth Wright, aged thirty-two, single mother of one. A

known user and is on the system for being cautioned three times. Officers last had words with her five months ago, but the latest information we have on her is that she's been clean and trying to get her life back on track, or risk losing her seven-year-old boy for good."

"Why has she still got her kid? Surely, the boy is at risk?" Karen commented.

Belinda shrugged. "You would think so, wouldn't you? To begin with, social services got involved and took him into care for a while, but they were happy that she was in a better place. So, Bradley, her son, was returned to her only two months ago on a trial basis, with social services paying weekly visits. Then she had a relapse."

Karen tutted. In her mind, she believed they should never have returned Bradley and placed him in a vulnerable setting. She doubted he even attended school.

Karen turned on to Carter Avenue and saw several police cars and a forensic van ahead. She pulled on to the pavement and squeezed in between two cars before covering the short distance on foot with Belinda. It was a narrow street with barely enough space for two cars to pass each other, which is why residents double-parked on the pavement, leaving little space for her and Belinda to walk side by side. She wondered how mothers could push a pram down this road. It was a mixture of houses, all semi-detached, with many having well-maintained hedges round the border of their front gardens, while others had converted their gardens into front drives for their cars. It wasn't as bad as she'd been led to believe.

As she approached the house, several officers milled round while they watched forensic officers come and go. She signed in on the scene log and slipped on the provided blue booties and nitrile gloves.

Detritus lay strewn across the narrow footpath leading

to the peeling front door. It hung from its frame after officers had executed a forced entry following concerns from neighbours. Raising her hand to shield her face, she ducked under the police tape cordoning off the front door.

The stench hit them first—an overpowering, putrid reek that made their eyes water and stomachs lurch. Karen had encountered many crime scenes in her years as an officer, but the cloying miasma assaulting her nostrils hinted at something particularly squalid awaiting them.

Belinda stepped into the dim interior and on to the metal plates that the CSIs had positioned to avoid disturbing the scene.

Karen shook her head. If the hallway was anything to go by, then the rest of the house must have been a pigsty because empty drinks cans, biscuit wrappers, and chip packets lay discarded on the surrounding floor. The air inside was thick and stale, a noxious blend of staleness, human misery, and something hinting at rot.

Her hunch was right. The narrow hallway opened into dimly lit, claustrophobic rooms crammed with heaps of squalor. Piles of soiled clothes, boxes, newspapers, and indistinguishable filth blanketed every surface. Take-away containers crawling with insects intermingled with spent needles and crack pipes amid the sea of misery that lay discarded round them.

"Shit," Karen muttered under her breath as they picked their way towards the back room, her eyes struggling to decide where to land. The scene probably looked far worse because they had set up arc lights to illuminate the space where Izzy and CSIs worked.

There, amid the overwhelming chaos, a prone figure lay face down on the grubby carpet. Matted dyed-blonde hair fanned out beneath the woman's head, thick streaks of congealed blood snaking across the dirty strands.

"Jesus," Belinda said as she exhaled. "I'll speak to the officers to see what else they've found."

Karen nodded but didn't reply as she crouched beside the victim. A young child's defaced pencil drawing of a sunny garden scene with a swing and brightly coloured flowers lay crumpled and forgotten beneath the woman's outstretched hand. There was so much more to the drawing as she examined the stick figures of a child and adult side by side, holding hands.

The stench of death, long present but sharpening by the second, revealed this house's grim secrets. Karen felt the familiar pangs of sorrow, anger, and grim determination harden her resolve as she took in the heart-rending scene.

"Morning, Karen. Someone has done a right number on her," Izzy commented as she sat back on her heels.

"What have you found so far?"

"Repeated blunt force trauma. There's no evidence of penetrative wounds to the body or sexual assault. Someone battered her round the head... And didn't stop until she was dead."

"Time of death?"

Izzy tilted her head to one side as she thought about it. "Within the last twelve hours. So, during the night."

"Okay, thanks. Any idea when you'll do the PM?"

"I'll slot her in first thing tomorrow morning if that works for you? I'm up to my eyeballs today in paperwork and reviews."

Karen nodded. She left Izzy to it and went in search of Belinda, finding her in a grubby kitchen towards the rear.

"How do people live like this?"

Belinda shook her head. "I've seen this far too often. Neglected, let down by those who are supposed to help them, and addictions. It's a recipe for disaster."

"Where's Bradley?"

"Back in the care of social services. He hasn't been here for over a month. Upon the last visit, they deemed that his mother was unfit to look after him, and despite her protests and promises to get herself sorted again, they had to do the right thing."

"They must have seen the state of this place on their last visit?"

"Yes. Beth's case was under review. They knew she wasn't coping and had plans to move her and get the help she needed, but she refused. They were unable to take any action other than forcibly removing her against her will."

"Bloody tragedy. Boyfriend? Husband? Next of kin?"

Belinda referred to her notes. "No boyfriend or husband. Well, not at present anyway. We're not sure where she was getting her gear from. Perhaps a dealer did this to her? Couldn't pay up, so he battered her." She checked her notes again. "We don't know who Bradley's father is, and her last boyfriend, John Henry, is known to us. He's a burglar and shoplifter. He completed a three-year sentence and was released eight months ago, but we have no information about his current location."

"Was he violent towards her?"

"He has a history of violent assault. We need to find him first. Beth's mother lives on the other side of town."

Karen sighed. "Okay, let's pay her a visit. Let me call Zac to tell him I'll be late." She pulled her phone out of her pocket and stepped away for some privacy.

"Hey, you," Karen said when Zac answered.

"Hey, lover, you okay?"

"Yes. I've had a job come in. Suspicious death in Tang Hall. Female, single mother of one and a user. I think it's going to be a late one. I need to visit her next of kin."

"Okay, keep me posted. I'll be at home all day anyway. Ton of case files to review."

"Will do. Love you, Zac."

"Love you, too."

Karen cut the call and made her way back to her car with Bel in tow.

5

Zac checked the time on his phone and let out a weary sigh. It was gone six p.m., and he still had a mountain of work to plough through before he could call it a night. The afternoon had flown by in a blur as he'd reviewed each case file, marking up the next points of action his team needed to take to progress the investigations. Rubbing at his sore, gritty eyes with the heels of his palms, he sank back against the sofa cushions and let out a sigh.

Karen still hadn't called with an update on her plans, and with Summer staying with her mum, he suspected it would be dinner for one, a microwave meal. He hauled himself to his feet with a groan and trudged through to the kitchen, yanking open the fridge and snatching out one of the ready meals that were always a quick and easy standby. Carbonara, not his favourite, but it would do. Zac's stomach made a rumbling noise as he pierced the plastic film with a fork a few times before quickly putting the whole thing into the microwave.

He watched the microwave's digital timer count down the last seconds, tapping his fingers restlessly on the worktop. At last, the shrill chime of the microwave timer pierced the heavy silence. He snatched up a tea towel and pulled open the microwave door, recoiling slightly as a waft of scorched plastic and sodium-laden steam billowed out. Not quite the most appetising aroma, but needs must. He carefully extricated the blistering hot plastic tray and set it down on the counter to cool for a few minutes before eating.

Turning back to the fridge with a yawn, he grabbed himself a beer—a crisp, cold bottle of Beck's would be the perfect accompaniment to this distinctly underwhelming evening's meal. But before he could even close the fridge door, the chime of the doorbell interrupted him. Zac paused, cursing whoever was disturbing him at this hour as he closed the fridge and set his beer down next to his sad-looking carbonara container.

He padded up the hallway and peered through the peephole. An overweight man wearing a grey T-shirt with the Amazon logo on the left chest and blue jeans, stood holding a small Amazon box. He was staring at the handheld device they all carried. This must be the car care products he'd ordered, Zac thought.

Zac pulled open the front door, mouth open and ready to greet the delivery driver, but the words stalled in his throat. Zac recoiled in shock, his cry of alarm fading on his lips as six hulking figures clad head to toe in black appeared from the side and stormed through the open doorway, a torrent of stomping boots and raised handguns filling the cramped hallway.

Black balaclavas obscured their faces as they set upon him, forcing him to cower under a torrent of punches and kicks. Wiry yet strong arms and fists mercilessly pummelled him, slamming him back against the wall. Zac's mind raced as he glimpsed the panic button mere feet away, its red surface gleaming like a beacon of hope. If he could just reach it...

With a burst of adrenaline, Zac surged forward with his shoulder dropped, pushing through and past two of the assailants. Their surprised grunts spurred him on. He stretched out his arm, fingertips straining towards the button. For a fleeting moment, hope swelled in his chest. Just a little further... and help would arrive in minutes.

Just when his finger reached the plastic, rough hands grabbed at him from behind. Strong fingers dug into his flesh, yanking him back with brute force. Zac twisted and turned, throwing punches blindly, desperate to break free. His knuckles connected with solid flesh, eliciting another grunt of pain. A small victory, but short-lived, and their agony turned to fury.

They swarmed him, their sheer numbers overwhelming. Their reckless violence unrelenting. A fist slammed into Zac's jaw, snapping his head back, the coppery taste of blood filling his mouth. Stars exploded across his vision, bright and disorienting. He staggered, his legs giving way beneath him.

They sent him crashing to the floor with bone-jarring force, the hallway floor unforgiving beneath his battered body. Pain exploded through Zac as they battered him from all sides, boots connecting with his ribs, his stomach, his face. He struggled, flailing and kicking, trying to fend off the blows, desperate to get to his feet and make another attempt for the panic button, but he was outnumbered and weakening against their brute force. Each blow sapped his strength, his resolve.

The panic button taunted him, so close yet impossibly out of reach, a mocking reminder of how close he'd come to calling up help. As the relentless assault continued, Zac's world narrowed to a haze of pain and the sinking realisation that no one was coming to save him. No reinforcements charging to his rescue. He was on his own, at the mercy of these faceless attackers, their intentions as dark as the clothing they wore.

Through swollen eyes, Zac caught a glimpse of a raised boot, poised to strike.

"I'm a police officer!" he choked out between ragged gasps, desperate for them to stop this brutal assault. "Stop!"

His words fell on deaf ears. Or perhaps they simply didn't care.

He braced himself for the impact, knowing that it could very well be the blow that finally sent him spiralling into oblivion. And as the boot descended, he couldn't help but wonder if this was how it all ended—not in a blaze of glory, but in a brutal, senseless attack in the supposed safety of his own home.

The impact left him reeling as his head tipped back and slammed against the floor. Pain flooded his body. Nausea swirled in the pit of his stomach, and his vision blurred.

Within seconds, someone threw a coarse black hood over his head, thrusting him into a terrifying, obliterating darkness. He gasped for air, panic clawing at his throat as a heavy knee slammed into his chest, pinning him down as multiple pairs of hands seized his wrists and ankles in an iron grip. Grunts and shouts echoed round him as his attackers barked harsh, unintelligible orders to one another amidst the chaos. Zac's attackers swiftly choked off his muffled screams of terror and abruptly hauled him upright. They frogmarched him through the front door, while he thrashed wildly as his socked feet slid uselessly across the ground, unable to gain any traction.

He yelled out as his toes slammed against the pavement outside, the rough concrete scraping and bruising them, but the more he resisted the more aggressive his captors became. This couldn't be happening. His panicked mind babbled over and over.

But the terror was real. Much too real. As Zac was hurled into a van, he realised with a lurch of dread that his fate was out of his hands. He was trapped in the enveloping blackness of the hood, his senses shot to pieces, bound and utterly helpless. He recognised the side door running along its rails before slamming shut. The crack of Zac's head against the unforgiving steel floor only confused him further as he lay on his side. Dazed from the vicious blows, his ears rang. As the engine roared in to life, tyres squealing in protest, Zac was thrown against the side wall.

In that moment, with the vehicle rapidly speeding up and carrying him off to some unknown fate, the full, and terrible gravity of his predicament struck home. He was being abducted by unknown assailants, his life literally resting in the callous hands of these merciless men. As a police officer, he should have been prepared for such an eventuality... but nothing could have braced him for this nightmare.

6

Jade's shoulders ached, and her legs felt stiff after sitting through a mind-numbingly boring training session for five hours. She could think of better ways to spend her afternoon, but it formed part of her PDP and was needed if she wanted to progress her career.

If that wasn't bad enough, she knew her cupboards were bare, so had stopped off at Sainsbury's for her weekly shop. Laden with two heavy bags that were straining at the handles, and her handbag slung over her shoulder, she trudged up the steps to her apartment. Though hungry, the only thing she looked forward to was a long, hot shower, throwing on her PJs, and getting into bed with her Kindle. Though work hadn't been busy in recent weeks, she was still late home most nights which didn't give her the opportunity to plough through her list of books that she had downloaded through her Kindle Unlimited membership.

She puffed out the last few steps before stopping at her front door and resting her bags on the floor. Fishing out her keys from her handbag, she slid the key into the lock and opened the door. *Home at last.*

The two Sainsbury's bags seemed heavier as she hauled them up and stepped into her hallway, placing the bags to one side before turning to shut the door. She gasped as her eyes grew wide. With little time to react, four men dressed in black, their faces covered with black balaclavas, rushed at her. The sheer force knocked her backward and she landed on the floor with a heavy thump. Jade screamed at the top of her voice before a man's hand muffled her mouth. She thrashed about on the floor, but they were too heavy for her. One man grabbed her arms and hoisted them above her head; another held her legs by the ankles.

A sickening dread washed over her. "Stop! I'm the police!" Jade screamed. One of the men aggressively hammer punched her in the stomach in response to her protest. The force pushed the air from her, forcing her to cough and splutter. Whoever they were, a police officer meant little to them, which made it worse.

Terror twisted her features as her face reddened. A house invasion. One of the most terrifying things a person could experience. Confusion clouded her thoughts as her eyes looked at the shadowy figures above her. In the darkness of the hallway, it was impossible to make out any of their features let alone the colour of their skin. This was it. *Was she about to be raped or killed?* The harder she tried to wriggle the more forceful they became. A stinging slap to her face shocked her to the core, paralysing her body. Before she had the chance to process anything else, rough hands pinned her arms down while something coarse and stifling was yanked over her head, plunging her into total blackness. She tried to scream, but a meaty hand clamped over her mouth, muffling her cries.

Her chest heaved with panicked breaths, each inhale filling her lungs with stale cotton fibres. She could taste the salty tang of old sweat soaked into the hood's fabric as it clung to her lips and assaulted her nostrils. The claustrophobic cocoon stole her vision and threatened to suffocate her.

The whole thing seemed to go on for minutes, but in reality, it was no more than a few seconds as they hoisted her to her feet and dragged her from her apartment. A neighbour on the same landing came out to see what the commotion was about and screamed when one man held a handgun up and told her to go back inside. The woman rushed back in without needing to be told twice.

Jade's feet clattered on the stairs as her mind reeled and spun. They were part lifting and part dragging her down the flight of stairs.

"Stop!" Jade begged, but a punch to the side of her head left her dazed and in pain. As Jade was shoved into the back seat of the vehicle, she could feel the chilly night air creeping through her clothes. Her heart pounded so hard that she could feel it reverberating in her skull. Two men held her in place before the car accelerated off at speed. But it wasn't just one car. She heard another roaring away behind her.

Suddenly, muffled voices up front—male tones growling indistinctly—filled the air. Accents she didn't know. A throaty chuckle penetrated the roar of the engine. Jade's skin crawled as it triggered visions of leering faces hiding beneath balaclavas, jeering at her helplessness.

Jade knew if she had any chance of escaping this nightmare alive, she needed to regain control and rely on her training. With effort she forced air into her lungs through clenched teeth. As the vehicle slowed slightly, she strained her ears, determined to glean any clues that could help her understand what was happening.

She gulped frantic breaths, her chest spasming with stifled sobs of panic. Dread and fury twisted in her gut as the terrifying reality led to the knowing that she was trapped, kidnapped, being taken to God knows where against her will.

7

The address for Beth's mum took Karen and Belinda less than thirty minutes as they snaked their way across town. As Karen drove, the image of that child's drawing flashed in her mind and though she pushed it away, it kept coming back. Such a simple depiction of happy family life through a child's eyes, which in no way resembled the reality. Throughout her career, she had confronted similar domestic situations. Losing a job, a marriage ending, or even the pressure of not being able to pay the bills or feed the family, led to a breakdown of normal family life. And that was often the catalyst that led to lives spiralling out of control.

Neither her nor Belinda were fully aware of Beth's situation and what had led to her life being ended in such tragic circumstances, but it was the children in these situations that upset her the most.

Karen slowed her car as they neared the address. "Certainly a marked contrast to where we've just been," Karen commented. The roads were wider, the houses though still semi-detached, were larger, well-maintained, and the entire area had a less intimidating feel.

Belinda nodded as she stared out of her passenger window. Clean frontages, nicer cars.

Karen parked across the drive and together with Belinda, they walked up the path. Two squares of grass bordered each side. She rang the doorbell and waited. From somewhere within, footsteps approached.

A thin, well-presented woman with dark brown hair and dressed in jeans and a cream jumper answered. Her eyes darted between the two visitors standing on her doorstep.

"Gillian Wright?" Karen asked.

The woman's eyes narrowed before she nodded. "Yes, that's me." Her voice was soft and clear.

"I'm Detective Chief Inspector Karen Heath from York police, this is my colleague Detective Constable Belinda Webb," Karen said as she held up her warrant card. "May we come in for a moment? It's about your daughter Beth."

Gillian's features changed. A look of concern replaced a small smile as her face paled. She nodded before showing them through to the lounge, a clean and contemporary space with beach effect laminate flooring, grey sofas, and a few decorative prints on the wall. As Karen glanced round, she noticed there were no pictures of Beth and just a few of Bradley.

"Has something happened?" Gillian asked as she offered the officers a seat and took the armchair opposite them.

Karen confirmed Beth's details and address with Gillian before continuing. "I'm really sorry to give you some bad news, but we found your daughter dead this morning at her home. We are treating it as murder."

Gillian's face became ashen as her eyes grew wider.

She glanced down at the floor and wrapped her hands into a ball in her lap. Karen noticed Gillian whisper something soft which sounded like the words of a prayer.

"What happened?"

"We are still gathering evidence, but we were called to the address an hour ago following a call from concerned neighbours."

Gillian looked up; her eyes were wide with concern, a hand on her chest. "Bradley?"

"As far as we know, he is safe. He's in the care of social services and wasn't at the property. We can arrange for you to see him?"

Gillian nodded, but pursed her lips. There was a pained and saddened expression in her eyes as she looked round the room, stopping on Bradley's photo.

"When did you last speak with Beth?" Belinda asked.

Gillian sighed and shook her head. "We haven't spoken in many months. Each time I try to contact her, she rejects me. But I still tried. I was concerned for Bradley and as his grandmother wanted to see him. We drifted apart many years ago when she fell in with the wrong crowd, and despite my efforts to help, she pushed me away, choosing those who injected her with that poison, over the love of her own mother."

Karen and Belinda exchanged a glance. Karen had heard this same sad story so many times, and although she was hardened to it, she felt desperately sad for any family experiencing it. She asked a few more questions before Gillian sobbed into her hands. Belinda left the lounge to make Gillian a cup of strong tea before returning a few moments later. Gillian thanked her and cupped the mug in her hands.

The more Karen listened, the more tragic the tale became. Caught up in a drug-fuelled life, Beth could not look after herself, let alone her son. Not that she came from a dysfunctional family. Though Beth's father had died when she was very young, her mother had done everything possible to give her a safe and loving home life, including good schooling, church on Sundays, and Brownies and Guides.

"We understand she was involved with John Henry. Do you know if he was back in her life again?"

Gillian looked up from her mug and shook her head in Karen's direction. "I don't. I was aware of his existence, but never laid eyes on him. Even though I visited Beth's place numerous times, she hardly ever opened the door to me, even though I was aware she was inside. I heard a man's voice through the letter box. Perhaps that was him?"

It was unlikely that Karen would get any answers to progress her investigation, which frustrated her. Finding John Henry needed to be her starting point.

Karen rose from the sofa and walked over to the picture of Bradley. He looked like a soft, sweet, and happy boy, with a cheeky smile that revealed he had lost a tooth at the front. "I understand that this will be challenging for you, but we will need you or another member of your family to complete a formal identification. We can arrange for a family liaison officer to take you."

Gillian nodded. "When?"

"The sooner the better. There'll be a post-mortem tomorrow, so we need a formal identification before that."

Gillian rose from the sofa and nodded. "Okay. Let me get myself sorted."

As Gillian headed upstairs, Karen and Belinda made their way back to the front door to wait outside for the FLO that Belinda was now arranging. It was while they were outside that both of their radios erupted into a flurry of garbled messages. Neither of them had time to comprehend the entirety of them as they both froze on the spot.

Karen's body trembled, her hand barely able to grasp the radio as she listened. She felt her legs turn to jelly. Belinda threw a hand over her mouth as she gasped. The force-wide alert went out to all available officers. Zac and Jade had been abducted. Karen couldn't think straight, her mind in meltdown. Had she heard correctly? It had been a long day. Had she misunderstood the message?

"Shit!" Belinda shouted. "Fuck! Fuck!" she blurted out as she ran a hand through her hair.

Karen didn't know what to do. Where should she go? Who needed her more? She never dreamt that she would find herself in this situation, and there was no protocol for it. A blind panic stole her senses as her hands became clammy and a sheen of perspiration covered her forehead. Her stomach retched. She turned and raced to the bushes before throwing up and dropping to her knees.

"Karen... Karen, we need to go. Now!" Belinda barked as she grabbed Karen's shoulder.

Karen blinked and wiped her lips with the back of her hand. This couldn't be happening. "I need to go to Zac's. Can you go to Jade?"

Belinda nodded. "You take your car, and I'll get a patrol car to pick me up. Go!"

Karen fumbled for her keys before rising and staggering to her car. There were so many questions swimming round in her mind but none of them made sense as she started her car and drove off. She wanted to yell. She wanted to cry. She wanted to know why?

8

Sirens wailed all round Karen as she raced back towards Zac's house, the insistent screech of the police sirens seeming to drill right into her skull. Flashing blue lights whizzed past in a dizzying blur. She had never encountered anything similar to this, and it seemed as if every police car in the country had arrived in York. The entire journey was a blur, and she remembered little of it as she approached Zac's road. The questions came in a steady stream, bouncing round in her brain, confusing and overwhelming her. One minute she was thinking about Zac, and the next Jade.

What happened to both of them? Who abducted them?

As she drove, there was a constant chatter on the radios about vehicles that may have been involved and eyewitness accounts. It sounded catastrophic, a scene of controlled chaos that made Karen's blood run cold. She gasped and had to force down the wave of nausea that scorched the back of her throat when the unmistakable word "firearms" crackled over the radio amidst the noise.

She pulled into Zac's road and slowed, her jaw dropping. Police cars lined the road for as far as she could see, their dazzling blue lights bouncing off the surrounding houses in an insane, strobing light show more befitting a disco than a residential area. She barely remembered to put the car into park before leaping out and didn't bother locking it as she grabbed her bag and raced towards Zac's house. Neighbours gathered on the pavements and in their front gardens, faces etched with shock and concern as they took in the swarming police presence. More armed officers than Karen could count huddled in groups outside Zac's home, MP5 sub-machine guns draped across their chests.

Detective Superintendent Laura Kelly barked orders to her officers as she coordinated the scene. She caught sight of Karen sprinting towards her, chest heaving, and held up a hand to halt her before Karen careened headlong into an active crime scene.

"Ma'am, what happened?" Karen panted, running trembling fingers through her hair as she looked towards Zac's house in desperation. "Where is Zac?" Karen's breath was laboured as she looked over Kelly's outstretched arms that stopped Karen from running closer to the scene. CSIs lingered in the doorway examining the scene, the flashbulbs from their cameras lighting up the hallway.

Kelly pursed her lips as she filled Karen in on the scant details they had so far. "We don't know, Karen. Eyewitness accounts confirm two vehicles, a white van, and a black Mercedes. At least six men, maybe more, dressed in black with black balaclavas forced a way into Zac's house and abducted him. At gunpoint."

Karen rested her hand on her forehead as she stumbled back a few paces, head swimming. Her knees threatening to buckle beneath her frame. She took in her surroundings. Police vehicles crowded the street, the heavily armed officers stood grim-faced with fingers poised on the triggers of their guns, and the murmured consternation from Zac's shocked neighbours. A crime scene of unspeakable violence, and Zac at the very heart of it.

"Karen, was Zac alone? Or did he have his daughter staying over?"

Karen's eyes widened and her mouth dropped open. *Summer!* Thank God Summer wasn't in the house. She would need to be told, but how? Karen had no idea what to say to her without alarming her. And it was something she would prefer to do in person, but she doubted Kelly would let her.

"No, ma'am. Summer is with her mum for a few days. Zac would have been alone."

"Right. Leave it with me. I'll follow up."

"Footage?" Karen croaked out, feeling as though her throat had been raked with sandpaper. "CCTV? We must have caught them on camera somehow, surely?"

Kelly nodded. "We've recovered the footage from Zac's house and from neighbours. We are reviewing them now."

"Panic button? Why didn't he hit the panic button? It's right by the bloody door."

Kelly shook her head. "I've reviewed the footage so far; Zac didn't stand a chance. He answered the door and before he had time to react, six men piled in."

"Ma'am," she pleaded, hating how she sounded like a broken, cowering child instead of a hardened police officer but too distraught to care. "I need to see it. Please? I have to know…" It felt like her heart was being ripped out piece by piece. She had a feeling of helplessness and yet anger towards those who had done this.

Kelly held out her hands to calm Karen. "Not yet. We

need to work fast to find out what happened. But I know how distressing this is for you. You can go to the doorway and take a quick look inside… but that's as far as you can go for now, understood?"

Karen nodded before following Kelly to the doorstep. Officers paused and watched Karen as she passed. They held a respectful silence, understanding her pain. It was only when she reached the doorstep that her heart lurched.

But nothing could have prepared Karen for the gut-punch of horror that winded her as she reached the doorstep. Her hand flew to her mouth, fingers digging into her cheeks as Kelly caught her round the waist, the only thing keeping her upright as her legs threatened to give way. She wanted to cry, cry until there were no tears left, but she couldn't lose it completely in front of her colleagues. There would be time for that later.

She couldn't drag her eyes away from the blood splatters on the hallway floor, or the coats that once hung on the newel post, now scattered across the floor. The hallway runner carpet lay crumpled. She tried hard not to let her mind conjure up the scene in glorious technicolour when Zac was attacked. Her skin felt damp as a shiver crept down her spine. Her body bucked as a tornado of fear and anguish rushed through her.

Karen retched, scrambling away from the doorway and Kelly's supporting grip as her stomach emptied itself on the grass. Tears streaked her pale cheeks as she bent double, wrapping her arms round her belly as wave after wave of nausea rolled through her.

"What can I do?" Karen asked as she forced herself upright, chest heaving as she sucked in ragged gulps of the cool night air.

"Nothing at the moment. You're emotionally involved in this situation, so I'm taking charge. I need you back at the station for your own safety and protection. I've organised AFOs to take you. Whoever did this may have been after you and because you weren't here, they took Zac instead."

The thought had crossed Karen's mind, which only added to the tension building inside her head. "What happened at Jade's?"

Before replying, Kelly's grim expression spoke volumes. She said in a low murmur, "Pretty much the same. Four men barged in behind Jade and attacked her before they took her away. Her neighbour came out to see what the commotion was about. They threatened her at gunpoint before bundling Jade into a car and driving off. We're still waiting on concrete details of the vehicle, but it appears these two attacks were coordinated."

"This is my fault, isn't it?" she choked. "I've put them both in danger." Tears rolled from her eyes as she placed a hand over her face. She willed herself to hold it together in front of everyone, but the tidal wave of emotions swirling inside her were too much for her to cope with.

"We'll talk as soon as I get back. The guys over there," Kelly said, pointing towards more than a dozen AFOs, "are going to escort you in convoy. I'm not taking any risks. Both locations involved the use of firearms, and the severity of the attacks all point to the same conclusion— that this was pre-planned, and we are dealing with very dangerous individuals. Go."

Karen agreed, but there's one thing she hated more than anything else, and that was taking a back seat in any investigation. It went against every fibre of Karen's being to step back and let others take the reins. That it was Jade and Zac only made it more painful for her. She turned and headed for the group of officers. After this, would life ever be the same again? And though she wasn't a religious person, she would pray every minute of every day if it meant the safe return of both Jade and Zac.

9

Karen sat in Kelly's office with her head in her hands. Two AFOs stood in the hallway on Kelly's orders. Karen's team from the SCU loitered nearby desperate for news and itching to help.

She felt numb. In a matter of hours her entire world, the world she had dreamt of, had come crashing down round her. An organised and coordinated attack on two officers. Unheard of in her career. This was big. She stared at the ceiling and blew out her cheeks. It was like being in a goldfish bowl with everyone lurking round outside. Karen couldn't face them and sat in a chair with her back to them. Her eyes were sore and red from crying. How had she lost everything so quickly?

It must have been an hour, maybe longer, since she'd arrived back at the station. She needed to be doing something, anything. Her legs bounced up and down on the balls of her feet. A nervous and uncomfortable energy that was crying out to be used. All she wanted to do was to be out on the streets searching for the two most important people in her life.

"Karen."

Kelly's appearance jolted Karen from her thoughts. She placed a hand on Karen's shoulder. "How are you holding up?"

Karen shook her head and shrugged. "I don't know. I... don't know."

Kelly pulled up one of the visitor chairs and sat opposite Karen. She looked weary and tired. "We've got door-to-door enquiries being conducted along the whole of Zac's street. We've secured every piece of CCTV footage and I've instructed officers to begin door-to-door enquiries in neighbouring streets. I need to find out the timeline of the vehicles involved and the route that they took both before and after taking Zac. The same thing is being replicated at Jade's place."

Karen nodded, though every word had slipped past her awareness. Things were being said, but much of it didn't register with her.

Kelly studied her but remained silent for a few moments. Karen stared straight back at her willing her to say something. Anything.

"Karen, you are the common denominator in this. There is a reason both of them were taken. It's a message for you." Kelly paused. "Now, it could be a disgruntled criminal seeking revenge because you put him away, but we would be considering an OCG due to the number of individuals involved."

Karen closed her eyes and nodded.

"I've tasked officers to look at the Harman angle. That's one of the biggest OCGs in our area, and you and your team dismantled them. That wouldn't have gone down well with Harman or his associates."

Karen accepted that. They had already fired off a

warning shot when they had taken Summer's friend. Had they ramped up their intention to really hurt her?

"I'm also thinking it might have something to do with the Connells. We are aware of Sally Connell's presence in the country and intelligence reports indicate her intention to free her brother from prison. That is also another revenge angle we need to consider."

"If it's true that she is in cahoots with a Russian OCG, then she would certainly have the muscle," Karen said.

Kelly agreed and nodded. "I'm going to reach out to the NCA as we need help on this. I then have a meeting with the chief constable and ACC Damien Jackson, among others. As soon as I know more I'll let you know. I've also called Zac's ex-wife to get her up to speed. She wasn't too pleased about the situation or the precautions and cut the call before I could say everything. I suggest you give it another try. Perhaps you'll have better luck."

"Thank you, ma'am. I'm not sure it will help, but I'll call Michelle."

"Yes. Do that right away. I've deployed armed officers to be stationed outside her house." Kelly rose from her seat and disappeared through the crowd of officers gathered outside her office.

Karen took a large breath and closed her eyes to calm her racing heart. This would be a challenging call. She grabbed her phone from the floor beside her and dialled Michelle's number.

"Michelle, it's Karen here. I need you to listen. Is Summer anywhere near you?" There was a seriousness in her tone.

"No. She is upstairs in her bedroom. I've already had the news. Zac was kidnapped. What's actually happened? You better tell me the truth. And not one more word about what I can or can't do!"

Karen closed her eyes again. "Some men entered Zac's house and abducted him. A second group of individuals did the same at my sergeant's apartment."

"Oh my God!" Michelle snapped. "What? I don't understand? How? What happened? Who was responsible?"

Karen couldn't cope with Michelle's demands. "Michelle, I don't have any answers for you at the moment. It's an active investigation as my colleagues work hard to track down where they both are. Because of my closeness to both of them, I'm not in charge, so I have few details."

Michelle remained silent, but Karen heard her heavy breathing.

"You won't like this, but until we identify why they were abducted, my boss has arranged for armed officers to be stationed outside your house as a precautionary measure. It's for your own safety."

"You are bloody joking. Are you telling me that me and my daughter are in danger?" she snapped.

"I don't think so. But we need to remain vigilant. For the time being, you and Summer need to stay indoors until you hear from us again."

"I'm not going to be forced to stay inside my house all the time. If I want to go out, I will bloody go out."

Karen wanted to scream down the phone, but what good would that do? "Please, bear with us. Just do as I ask. If you are not worried about yourself, please do it for Summer. You need to explain the situation to her, and I will call Summer when I get a chance. This is serious, Michelle. I mean it." The gravity in her voice was enough to silence Michelle. She finally relented before hanging up.

Karen wanted to be with Summer, holding her tight to

protect her. It wasn't fair on the poor girl after everything she had been through recently. With her still having nightmares about the abduction of a friend, and her reluctance to be out and about on her own for too long, Karen only wondered what further damage it would cause.

10

Karen spent the entire night sitting in her office, feeling tired and exhausted, the time dragging on with no news. She went from moments of clock-watching to pounding one fist into her palm as desperation turned to anger. It was the not knowing if they were both safe that was killing her. Officers worked throughout the night, with further reinforcements brought in from other stations. It was busier last night than it was during most day shifts. But it didn't offer her any reassurance. One minute she was crying, the next she experienced a burning urge to do anything to find them, only to slide down the wall of her office and tuck her knees into her chest as she stared at the emptiness surrounding her.

This morning was no different. Her heart raced, her mouth felt tinderbox dry, and the tightness in her chest was strangling her breathing. Another team had been reassigned the Beth Wright case. Kelly was insistent that with Karen being held within the confines of the station, she could not carry out her duties as the senior investigating officer in the woman's suspicious death.

Karen rose from her chair. She needed to take a shower. Thankfully, she stored a few spare sets of clothes in her cupboard. Throughout her career, she'd learned a valuable lesson from pulling overnighters. You couldn't always go home to have a shower, freshen up, and throw on a fresh set of clothes. It always made sense to have some spare in the office. She grabbed her shower bag and headed off. Officers nodded out of concern as she passed. Hushed conversations were taking place behind closed doors. With the lives of two officers on the line, this would be a situation that her superiors would want to resolve in hours rather than days.

The spray of hot water prickled her skin as Karen bowed her head in the shower. She closed her eyes and let the water massage her aching body. Frustration still gnawed away at her. Kelly wouldn't let her get involved because of her connection with both officers. That was understandable, but for someone like Karen, she hated nothing more than being relegated to the subs bench. Jade was her best friend and would put her life on the line for her. Zac... Zac was something else. There were instances when you meet someone and an instant connection was formed. You feel at ease with them, as if you've been lifelong companions, and you can be your true self without any pretence. That was what Zac meant to her.

Even in this darkest moment, a small smile spread across her face as she remembered a deep and meaningful conversation she'd had with Zac recently. It was a genuine heart-to-heart that Zac had completely spoiled when he'd mentioned that true love was when you no longer needed to hold your farts in. Then, he'd let one rip.

Karen stepped out of the shower, dried herself off, and slipped into new clothes, before standing in the mirror to dry her hair. "I look like shit," she muttered. Dark circles round her eyes, sagging jowls, and red lattice veined eyes. She sighed. At least she felt clean and fresh.

During the course of the night, Kelly had updated her following officers' ongoing review of CCTV footage. The results had only confirmed everyone's suspicions that this was a targeted attack when they'd found that the abductors had scoped out both properties several times in the days before the abductions. Descriptions were still vague, probably deliberate, bearing in mind CCTV footage was grainy and sketchy at best during the night. Combined with dark clothing, it made identifying suspects impossible. The team needed to focus on identifying the vehicles as their sole lead.

She went via the canteen and picked up two slices of toast and a strong black coffee before returning to her office. Though she wasn't hungry, she knew she needed to eat, but the way she felt meant there was a distinct possibility her food would come straight back up again. Her stomach turned like a slowly revolving cement mixer which sent waves of nausea through her.

A knock on a door startled her. Her senses felt frayed, fatigued, and slow. DI Anita Rani stood there, a warm smile on her face and a softness in her eyes. "Hey, you. I thought I'd get in early to see how you are?"

"I wish I had an answer for that," Karen said as Anita came in and hovered by her desk, before bending to give her friend a shoulder hug. Karen welcomed the friendship and connection. Although there were likely more than a hundred officers in the building and a heightened level of busyness, she had never experienced such a feeling of isolation.

"I understand. I can't imagine what you're going through. Is there anything I can do to help?"

"Not really, Anita. But thank you. I really mean that."

"You only have to ask. You do know that, don't you?"

Karen nodded. Before she could say anything, she saw Kelly through the glass frontage of her office. Behind followed DCI Shield. Normally, she would have groaned, but she was running on empty and felt indifferent about him.

Kelly and Shield turned and entered Karen's office.

Anita took a step back. "Ma'am, sir." They both nodded at her.

Karen stared at both in anticipation, searching their eyes for any news. Her hands balled into fists in preparation.

"How are you feeling, Karen?" Kelly asked.

"Holding up, ma'am. I feel helpless sitting around."

"Understandable," Kelly nodded. "I've appointed DCI Shield to be SIO in this case. I trust him."

"Ma'am, I'd like to be involved. I know what you said, but that only makes me more determined than ever to find them. Despite my relationship with both of them, we have two of our officers who have been abducted, so it definitely makes sense for every available officer, including me, to participate in the search."

Kelly shook ahead. "I hear what you're saying, but I can't have you leaving this building. Of course, yes, you could handle elements of the case while still being here, but on this occasion I need clear heads all round."

Karen understood that Kelly's hands were tied, and although she didn't have a liking for Shield, she recognised his determination to pursue those responsible. "But ma'am..."

Kelly held up a hand to silence Karen. "There are no buts this time."

Shield stuffed his hands in his pockets. "Listen, Karen, I know we've not seen eye to eye, and you're not my favourite person, but I'm trying to put those differences to one side. I'd like you to do the same." His voice was firm and directive. "You need to stay put here and leave me to get on with my job. It would only get complicated and messy if you were involved, and I'm sure the super wouldn't want to see her two top DCIs having a spat in public in front of all the other officers." He looked towards Kelly, who nodded.

Karen let out a deep sigh, her chest rising and falling. A prickly atmosphere lingered in the room. She finally nodded before resting her elbows on the table and burying her head in her hands.

"Right, let's get moving," Kelly said, before marching out of the office with DCI Shield and DI Anita Rani following behind.

11

Jade shivered, her whole body wracked by uncontrollable tremors as the damp, biting chill seemed to seep into her bones. The thin cotton of her top provided little to no insulation against the creeping cold, leaving her skin prickled with goosebumps. Her teeth chattered as she pulled her knees tighter together, trying to conserve what little warmth remained inside.

Her wrists burnt from the sharp plastic biting into her soft flesh as she tugged at the cable ties binding her hands behind her back. Her arms were contorted in an awkward, agonising position, providing no give or respite. The rough hood remained cinched over Jade's head, blocking out any trace of light or visual cues as to her surroundings. The overwhelming odour of mildew, decay, and damp earth saturated the cloying air trapped inside the hood.

Where was she? Perhaps an old warehouse? An underground chamber or tunnel?

Jade's heart hammered against her ribcage as she strained her senses, searching in vain for any noise that might give her a clue of where her captors were. But there was nothing except the ragged whistle of her own shallow breathing filling the confining hood, each exhale hot and humid against her sticky face.

She squirmed in the chair, trying to ease the cramps already seizing her muscles from the unnatural position she was bound in. But the simple movement only intensified the agony shooting through her shoulders and arms. A pitiful whimper slipped past her cracked lips as the ties bit deeper into her numb, sore wrists, a trickle of warm blood oozing down her fingers.

A wave of exhaustion and dehydration washed over Jade as sour nausea burbled up her throat. She retched dryly. The violent convulsion triggered a renewed flood of pain across her stomach from the savage blows that had started this nightmare.

Her mind replayed those harrowing moments—the men appearing out of nowhere, the brutal attack, the chaotic car journey here, and then another beating when she'd resisted efforts to restrain her in the chair. Questions raced through her mind. She wondered how long she had been trapped here. Time was irrelevant. Was it day or night outside? Were her captors watching from the shadows even now, enjoying her helpless suffering?

No... I can't let them see me scared. She balled her fists and gritted her teeth against the despair creeping in. She was stronger than this—more determined than whoever these unhinged psychopaths were that thought they could break her. Shutting out the surroundings as best she possibly could, Jade closed her eyes and focused on steadying her ragged breaths. But breathing was hard. Her face had dried tears clinging to it, her nose was blocked with snot, and her lips were cracked. Everything hurt.

Footsteps! At first, they were faint, little more than a

distant vibration against the uneven ground. But they grew louder, closer, echoing off the cavernous expanse until Jade could sense a looming presence mere feet away. She braced herself, every muscle tensed as taut as tightly coiled steel cables, pulse pounding with a surge of adrenaline-fuelled fight or flight instincts.

A man's hand reached under the hood, pulled it off, and shone a torch in her face. Jade's eyes flickered from the burning light searing her retinas. She flinched away with a strangled cry of shock and pain, blinking and squinting to force her eyes to focus. It took a few seconds to register where she was. A cavernous darkness. An underground chamber? Or a cave? It felt cold enough to be either. She spotted a few lights dotted about the place, which offered little in the way of illumination, but more a path to navigate the space.

Jade craned her neck and peered up at the ominous silhouette towering over her. Her mouth set itself in a taut, grim line when she saw the familiar dark shape of a balaclava shielding the man's features, only his eyes visible as cruel pinpricks of reflected torchlight.

Jade yelled. "Who are you?"

Silence.

"I'm a police officer. I demand that you release me at once."

Nothing.

Then a faint ripple of laughter echoed out from deeper within the cold, dripping space. Low and mocking, the sound of it sent an icy shiver ricocheting down Jade's spine that had nothing to do with the chill. They were laughing at her, getting some sick sadistic pleasure from her helpless terror.

"What do you want?"

No reply.

Jade coughed, spitting out a fresh lump of spittle and phlegm that had been clogging her airways. Even with every breath tasting of damp stone and mould, she could still detect the faint but unmistakable acrid reek of tobacco smoke somewhere out in the stillness. Not your usual Benson & Hedges or Silk Cut though—the aroma was far too strong and pungent, hinting at a Continental brand or roll-up cigarette.

"You want drink?" The man asked.

Jade blinked hard, trying hard to distinguish any features of the man as he lowered and angled his torch away from her face. His English was hesitant but gruff, stained by a thick rasp that suggested years of chain-smoking. European? The Balkans? She wasn't sure. Jade nodded.

The man held the lip of a bottle on Jade's lips and she took a few sips to quench her thirst. It was cold, icy-cold, which did little to warm her body. She shivered. "I'm cold," she croaked.

"Good," he grunted, no hint of empathy. Another mocking ripple of laughter echoed through the vast cavern, bouncing back from unseen recesses.

"Please," Jade pleaded, teeth chattering. "I'm freezing..."

He ignored her as he turned and disappeared into the darkness, speaking in a dialect that Jade wasn't familiar with.

The man returned with the torch now aimed towards the floor. Jade took a moment to study the ground round her. Uneven black stone and dirt. A fine dirt. The only conclusion she could come up with was that she was in a cave. Fuck!

"Soon," the man growled before turning and melting away into the darkness.

"Soon? What does soon mean? Wait... what?" Jade shouted. "What's happening soon?"

There was no reply, which only terrified Jade further. *Soon to be released? Soon to be killed?* Tears rolled down her face as she sobbed.

12

As Shield delivered an update to the team, Karen made her way to the back of the briefing room and settled herself in a seat. She hated the fact that he was up there, and she wasn't. Leading from the front was the one thing she wanted to do more than anything else. Kelly had snuffed out that chance. While she acknowledged the validity of her boss's reasons, it still hurt her to step back. The man she loved with all her heart was out there, the person who knew her better than anyone else, her best friend, was also out there, and somewhere deep within her, she couldn't shake the feeling that she was failing them both.

Karen's mind raced as she sat there, trying to focus on Shield's words but finding it impossible. Her thoughts kept drifting to Zac and Jade, imagining the horrors they might be facing at this very moment. She clenched her fists, her nails digging into her palms as a wave of frustration and helplessness washed over her. It took every ounce of her self-control to stay seated and not storm up to the front of the room, demanding more action, more urgency.

Over fifty officers were crammed into the briefing room, where it was standing room only. Shields stood at the front besides one of the incident boards. Pictures of Jade's apartment and Zac's house were pinned to them, along with stills taken from CCTV images of the shadowy figures and vehicles. Karen could deal with that, but it was pictures of Zac's hallway and the blood splatters that made her close her eyes. An icy chill ran down her spine as her imagination conjured up the worst possible scenarios. She shook her head, trying to dispel the dark thoughts, but they lingered like a heavy fog.

"How much progress have you made with door-to-door enquiries in neighbouring streets?" Karen blurted out, unable to contain herself any longer.

Shield paused in mid-flow and looked across the room at Karen. "We've covered it, and we have already logged any useful information on the system."

"We need to flood the area with more officers. What about dashcam footage? Some systems continue recording even when the car is parked. Have we looked at that avenue?"

Shield folded his arms across his chest and studied Karen for a moment. "DCI, with all due respect, this is my investigation, and I have allowed you to sit in. I appreciate what you're saying, and I know this is close to your heart and it's a very stressful time for you, but I don't need to be reminded on how to run this investigation."

Karen's jaw tightened as she glared at Shield. Her cheeks flushed as officers turned to stare at her. She couldn't help it. Overstepping the mark wasn't helping her situation but keeping quiet wasn't in her DNA. Karen pursed her lips and nodded before looking down at her fingers and playing with her nails. It was the lack of urgency that annoyed her. Perhaps she was being too harsh and critical. Deep down she knew they were doing everything in their power. All police leave had been cancelled. Kelly had drafted in specialist officers from HQ to help in the investigation, and specific directives from the chief constable needed to be implemented, one such action being the immediate need for a press conference.

As far as the chief constable was concerned, he wanted to put down as much publicity as possible, so his officers became too hot to handle. Karen only hoped that the CC was right. There was a possibility of it spooking the abductors and backfiring. She couldn't bear the thought of anything happening to Zac or Jade because of a misstep in the investigation. The weight of responsibility bore down on her, making it hard to breathe.

"Right, let's get back to what I was saying," Shield demanded. "I need ANPR alerts for the vehicles used in both abductions. Start with York city centre and move outwards. I want all main roads into and out of town checked and double-checked. Someone speak to the City CCTV Control Room too. Let's retrieve footage from their cameras for the night of the abductions."

Shield turned to the incident board and grabbed a black marker to add those points to the board. "Who is here from forensics?" He turned and studied the crowd. Two officers towards the rear raised their hands. "Where are we on the results from evidence obtained from both locations?"

One CSI checked her pad. "We've sent the blood samples away for comparative analysis, including a cross reference with DCI Zac Walker. Officers recovered clothing fibres from the hallway carpets at both residences, and a few also got snagged on the striking plate of the door latch at DCI Walker's property. We also picked up a few sets of prints on both front doors so far."

Shield nodded. "I doubt any of those prints will belong to our crew. Though the CCTV images are rough, it seems as if everyone was wearing gloves. They were pros. They weren't dicking about. Anything else recovered from both scenes?"

"No, sir."

"Composite photos?" he shouted next.

Another officer raised a hand. "We are working with the neighbour in the unit opposite DS Whiting's apartment. They came face to face with Jade's abductors. One of them pointed a gun at her face. It's slow-going because she is heavily traumatised, but we're working on creating an e-fit. The resident said that the man who held the gun had very dark angry eyes, was about five feet ten, thickset, and heavy, with a bit of a belly on him. The witness said the man had a thick foreign accent but couldn't say where from."

As the officer spoke, Karen's mind raced, trying to piece together any connections or clues that might lead them to Zac and Jade. She replayed every interaction, every conversation she'd had with them recently, searching for anything that might shed light on their abduction. But as much as she wracked her brain, nothing stood out. It was as if they'd vanished, leaving no trace behind.

Shield carried on with the briefing for another twenty minutes before bringing it to a close. As his officers rose to leave, he stopped them all. "Remember, we are dealing with very dangerous individuals who are heavily armed. We are not talking about wannabe gangsters or roadmen who hang about the estates acting hard and pretending to carry their bollocks round in wheelbarrows. Under no circumstances are you to go out alone on enquiries. You go out double crewed. Do I make myself clear?" Shield paused for a moment and studied the eyes of his officers as the gravity of the situation sunk in. "They threatened an innocent bystander with a gun. The next time, they might carry out their threat. If you come across anything suspicious... and I mean... *anything* suspicious, you call for backup and armed response. Now get out of here."

Karen filed out with the rest of the officers; she didn't want to be left alone in the room with Shield as he gathered his things together. She couldn't trust herself to keep her mouth shut. Her mind was already racing ahead, trying to figure out her next move. She knew she couldn't just sit back and wait for others to find Zac and Jade. She had to act, even if it meant going against protocol.

As she stepped into the hallway, Karen took a deep breath, steeling herself for whatever lay ahead. She knew the road would be long and difficult but was determined to bring Zac and Jade home safely, no matter the cost. With renewed determination, she set off down the hall, ready to face whatever challenges lie ahead.

13

WITHIN THE SPACE of a few hours, a press conference had been organised with reporters and journalists from all the major news channels across the country and local channels, newspapers, and online media outlets all congregated in the press room. This was a big story and one that was on the lips of every chief constable across the country. Though Karen wasn't privy to the information, she had heard through many officers that offers of support and resources had flooded in from every county.

Karen convened with her officers in the SCU. Those that weren't out on enquiries gathered round the TV, and where possible perched on desks and spare seats. Though Karen was the boss, she looked a lonely and desperate figure as she sat chewing her nails and staring straight at the screen. Her usual strong and assertive manner had long left, leaving her a shadow of her former self. The weight of the situation bore down on her, the uncertainty and fear for Jade and Zac's safety consuming her every thought.

Detective Superintendent Laura Kelly, DCI Shield,

and the chief constable sat behind a long table, with a big police banner behind them. To one side was a whiteboard with the two pictures of the missing officers. It pulled on Karen's heartstrings every time she saw their images. She shook her head in despair, fighting back the tears that threatened to spill over. She couldn't afford to break down, not now, not when Jade and Zac needed her to be strong.

The chief constable opened the press briefing by explaining the seriousness of the situation and led the whole show. Kelly chipped in, and DCI Shield discussed the coordinated effort underway to locate and safely bring home his colleagues. The CC took a moment to praise the professionalism of his team at such a difficult time, and touched on how both Jade and Zac were exceptional, kind, and well-respected officers who were an asset to his force. He urged members of the public to report anything suspicious, no matter how small or insignificant it might seem.

Karen leaned in as DCI Shield took over, her heart pounding in her chest. This was the moment Karen had been dreading, the moment when DCI Shield took over and laid bare the reality of the situation for all to see.

Shield cleared his throat. "I'm making a direct plea to members of the criminal community. I can't stress enough the seriousness of this situation, and I urge any of you who may be connected to it to come forward with any information. There is a fifty-thousand-pound reward for any information that directly leads to the safe return of these two officers. Disregard the fact they are serving police officers. They have families and friends who miss them and want them back." He paused and studied the audience, a steely cold look in his eyes which suggested he meant business.

Just his look was enough to intimidate most people,

and Karen imagined his stare was having the same effect on his audience as they remained quiet with not even the sound of shutters firing off on a camera. She hoped his words would reach the right people, that someone out there would have the courage to come forward and help bring Jade and Zac home.

He continued. "We are deploying every available resource visibly and covertly to find those responsible. We will leave no stone unturned, so I suggest that if you have any information relating to the abductions, that you come forward before it's too late as we will use every power at our disposal to bring all individuals involved to justice."

Karen noticed Kelly and the CC nod in agreement. Shield's speech had left the audience in silence for a few moments before the CC answered a flurry of questions at the end.

With the press conference over, Karen remained rooted in her chair staring at the blank monitor, trapped in her own little world, which was shrinking by the hour. She needed to stay positive. They had to find Jade and Zac. Having worked on cases involving abductions, the officers working this one had their work cut out for them. One thing worried her more than anything else. Whoever was responsible for this had access to firearms... a lot of firearms. It meant only one thing—they were serious and expected fatalities. The thought sent a chill down her spine, and she shuddered.

"We will find them." Claire placed her hand on Karen's shoulder as she came and stood behind her, startling Karen out of her dark thoughts.

"I hope so. I feel so bloody useless in here," Karen confessed, her voice just above a whisper.

"I can't imagine what you're going through." Claire,

with her voice soft and sympathetic, offered, "I'm always here if you want to talk."

Karen reached up and squeezed Claire's hand. "Thank you. It means a lot." Grateful tears welled in her eyes as she acknowledged the unwavering support of her team, each member wholeheartedly committed to bringing Jade and Zac home.

Ty, Preet, and Ned lingered close by and gathered round her as if protecting her in a cocoon. Their presence was comforting, and Karen felt a surge of affection for her team.

"They'll be back before you know it, and Jade will annoy you with her OCD and anti-bac lotions, and Zac will spoil you like he always does." Ned smiled as he stuffed his hands in his pockets.

Ned's comments were sweet and vulnerable, especially for him. He was often jittery and shy but, on this occasion, it felt like he was talking from the heart. Karen's eyes watered. Their kind words and concern overwhelmed her. She blew out her cheeks as her vision blurred, fighting back the tears that threatened to fall.

"Thanks, guys. You're all amazing. Now get on with the work and leave me alone to be a blubbering mess." They smiled as they left her alone, understanding her need for privacy at this difficult moment.

Karen rose from her chair in need of some solitude. She walked back to her office, her mind racing with thoughts of Jade and Zac. As she entered her office, her phone buzzed in her pocket. She scrambled to retrieve it and checked the screen with shaking hands. It was Brad. Please don't be calling me with bad news, she thought as she answered the call.

"Karen. I'm really sorry about what's happened to Jade

and Zac. I saw the press conference. Any news?" Brad spoke with concern in his voice.

Karen closed the door to her office and dropped into her chair, her legs suddenly feeling weak. "No, nothing yet. No leads other than grainy black-and-white CCTV footage. All we know at the moment is that whoever did this was heavy on numbers and big on firearms. That's a deadly combination," she said, her voice trembling.

"Yes. I wanted you to know that we are all thinking of you and if there's anything you need, you only have to ask," Brad said, his voice sincere.

There it was again. Support flooding in from everywhere. Each time it did, it felt like another stab in her heart. Her throat tightened with emotion. "Thank you. I will. When you see Steve, give him my love."

"Of course. Hey, listen, I can take a week's annual leave and come up. Or I can ask if they can transfer me to your team to help with the investigation, even if it's for a few days. I'd like to help."

Karen smiled despite herself. That was kind of him. "I appreciate that. I'll let DCI Shield know," she said, feeling a small glimmer of hope at the thought of having extra help on the case. Help that she knew well and trusted.

She hung up, tossed her phone on the desk, and leaned back in her chair. She closed her eyes and prayed for this nightmare to end... quickly. But even as she prayed, she knew that the road ahead would be long and difficult. She hoped that they would find Jade and Zac before it was too late. With a heavy heart, she opened her eyes and turned back to her computer, ready to dive back into the investigation with renewed determination. No matter what it took, she wouldn't rest until she found Jade and Zac.

14

Zac's mind raced as he struggled to make sense of his surroundings. They had removed the hood from his head, which was a troubling sign that his captors wanted him to see their faces. The dark, damp, and cold cave-like structure offered little comfort, with only a few scattered camping lights revealing the uneven, earthy stone walls. He sensed his captors lurking in the shadows, their dark clothing blending seamlessly with the darkness. They moved with a quiet, deliberate purpose, their conversations carried out in hushed tones and a strange, unfamiliar dialect that Zac couldn't quite place. Perhaps it was Eastern European, or even Russian.

The thirst and pain consumed him, his throat parched and his head throbbing with each passing moment. His body ached, a testament to the brutal surprise attack that had left him defenceless. The panic button by his front door, a direct link to the force control room, had been so close, yet out of reach. His eyes had shifted to the button during the attack, but there were too many of them to fight off. It all happened so quickly, mere minutes passing before they whisked him away, long before any help could arrive.

A spasm of pain shot up Zac's arm, causing him to groan in agony. The cable ties that bound his arms behind the chair were tight, nearly cutting off the circulation to his hands, which tingled and felt numb. He struggled against his restraints, desperate for any chance at escape, but his efforts proved futile.

Movement to his left caught Zac's attention, and he squinted into the blackness, trying to make out the shadowy figures gliding round him. "What am I doing here?" he shouted, his voice echoing in the cavernous space. Met with only silence and frustration, anger boiled up inside him. "I told you, I'm a police officer. You are in serious shit. You need to let me go." Still no response. "You fuckers! I know you can hear me. Unless you are deaf and fucking stupid!" Zac spat, clenching his fists as he wriggled in the chair, his desperation growing by the second.

"Every police officer in the county will be searching for you. How long do you think you can get away with this? You are all bloody crazy!" Zac's outburst finally attracted the attention of the men closest to him, one of whom marched over, his steps heavy and purposeful.

Zac was caught off guard by the first punch. It connected with his jaw and sent a wave of dizziness through his head. With the next two punches, his head jerked from side to side, sending shards of pain down his neck. The metallic taste of blood filled his mouth. Landing squarely on his temple, the fourth punch sent him into a temporary darkness. His head drooped forward, the pain behind his eyeballs pulsing as he regained consciousness. The ringing in his ears was deafening as he blinked, trying to focus on his surroundings.

The camping lights seemed to sway on invisible wires, adding to his disorientation.

Before Zac could fully gather his senses, another man grabbed a fistful of his hair, yanking his head back with brutal force. More dark figures emerged from the shadows, forming a menacing circle round him. A sense of dread settled in the pit of his stomach as he realised the gravity of his situation.

"Bastards!" Zac muttered through his swollen, bloody lips, summoning the last of his defiance to spit blood at the man standing before him.

And then the onslaught began. A relentless flurry of punches from all angles, connecting with his head and torso, each blow driving the air from his lungs and sending waves of agony through his battered body. They used him as a human punchbag, their faces devoid of any emotion, not a single laugh or word uttered as they methodically beat him.

When the attack finally ceased, they yanked his head back once more. Zac gasped for air, his body wracked with pain unlike anything he had ever experienced before. Through the haze of agony, he barely registered the noose being placed round his neck until it was too late. As it tightened, lifting him a few inches off the chair, he choked and gasped, his lungs burning for oxygen. The flash of a camera phone blinded him, capturing his torment. Another flash. And another.

Just as suddenly as it had begun, someone released the pressure and removed the noose. The figures melted back into the background, leaving Zac writhing in agony, blood trickling down his chin as he struggled to breathe.

Zac's mind reeled, trying to make sense of the torture he had just endured. What did they want from him? Why were they doing this? The questions swirled in his mind, mingling with the pain that consumed every fibre of his being. He thought of Karen, his colleagues, his friends, and his family. Were they looking for him? Did they even know he was missing? The uncertainty gnawed at him, almost as much as the physical pain.

As he sat there, alone in the darkness, Zac clung to the hope that someone would find him, that this nightmare would end. But deep down, he knew his chances were slim. These men, whoever they were, seemed to have planned this meticulously. They weren't amateurs. They knew what they were doing.

Zac closed his eyes, trying to block out the pain and the fear that threatened to overwhelm him. He focused on his breathing, each inhale and exhale a small victory against the agony that wracked his body. He had to stay strong, to hold on to the belief that he would make it out of this alive. But as the minutes ticked by and the shadows grew longer, that belief wavered.

In the cave's silence, broken only by his own laboured breathing, Zac prayed. He prayed for strength, for courage, and for a miracle. He prayed that somehow, against all odds, he would survive this ordeal and make it back to the people he loved. But even as he did, a small voice in the back of his mind whispered that this might be the end, that he might never see the light of day again.

With every passing moment, Zac felt his hope slipping away, replaced by a growing sense of despair. The pain, the isolation, and the uncertainty were taking their toll, chipping away at his resolve. He knew he had to fight and hold on to the belief that he would be found, but each passing second made it harder.

As he sat there, bound and broken, Zac couldn't help but wonder what his captors had in store for him next. Would they continue to torture him? Would they kill him?

The possibilities were endless, and each one more terrifying than the last.

But even in the depths of his despair, Zac refused to give up. He clung to the memories of his loved ones, to the knowledge that they would never stop searching for him. He found strength in their love and the belief that somehow he would be reunited with them.

And so Zac waited. He waited for the next blow, the next flash of pain, the next glimmer of hope. He waited for a chance, any chance, to fight back, to escape, to survive. And in the darkness of that cave, with nothing but his own thoughts for company, Zac made a silent promise to himself. He would not die here. He would not let these bastards win.

15

"Karen... Karen."

Karen jumped in her chair. Somewhere deep within her subconscious she heard a name being called. Her eyes shot open and scanned her surroundings as it took a few moments for her brain to engage. She rubbed her eyes. Shield hovered in the doorway.

"Sorry, must've fallen asleep. Shit." Karen grabbed her phone to check the time. She had been asleep for thirty minutes. She straightened up in her chair and shook her head to wake up.

"You're exhausted. Your body clearly needed a break," Shield replied.

"No... No, I can't sleep. How can I sleep when they're out there? I should be out looking for them."

Shield grunted and tutted. "You'd be of no use to man or beast in this state. You'd only get in the way."

Karen stiffened as her nostrils flared and her face reddened. She glared at Shield. *Keep calm and breathe.* She wasn't sure what it was about Shield that annoyed her so much. His arrogance? His brash attitude? Or whether he was simply an A1 dick from the school of dickheads, but he really got under her skin.

An awkward silence settled in the room with both officers looking away and examining her office. It was a while before Shield broke the silence. "I thought I'd give you an update before it went on the system. The door-to-door enquiries in neighbouring streets have recovered several hundred hours of footage from domestic CCTV and I have forty officers reviewing them. So far we have identified which direction all the vehicles were travelling in when they left Zac and Jade's places. We did, but we lost them after ten minutes of leaving Zac's, and thirteen minutes of leaving Jade's. But we are hoping to pick up their routes as we examine more footage from the council run cameras."

Karen grimaced. It was something, but still gave them little to go on.

"We've also recovered the burnt-out remains of three cars and a van. The registration numbers identified in the CCTV footage were false plates. We've tracked them back to the original vehicles and owners. All the plates were stolen less than twenty-four hours before the attacks. They were clever." Shield nodded. "They intentionally waited until the last moment so that even if the plates were reported for road traffic offences, it would take some time before we noticed them."

"Any forensics from them yet?" Karen asked.

Shield drew in air through his teeth and shook his head. "Nothing left of them other than twisted metal. Bart's team is working on them now."

Karen dropped her head in defeat. Things were moving, and any evidence offered little in the way of insights.

"Hey, listen. We need to stay positive. I..." Shield

paused. "I understand it's difficult for you, and I don't want to add to your challenges. But we are doing everything we can. I wanted to give you this update before I shared it with the team and got it on the system. Sorry I couldn't give you any good news."

Karen appreciated it and noticed a softening in his voice as he spoke to her. For a change he sounded sincere.

Shield continued. "I have a meeting with..." A chime on Karen's phone interrupted him.

Karen grabbed her phone and saw there was a WhatsApp message. She clicked open the message and froze; her eyes were wide with fear as her hands trembled. She gasped, not able to get air in quick enough as her lungs contracted. The phone slipped from her hand as she let out a blood-curdling scream. She gripped the sides of her head and clamped her eyes shut. "No! No!"

Officers came racing down the corridor from the SCU as Shield stepped forward and grabbed Karen's phone. He studied the image, then looked at Karen, then back at the phone. He blew out his cheeks as he ran a hand through his hair.

"Shit," he muttered as he turned to see more than a dozen officers crammed in the space by Karen's door. "Look after her," Shield shouted as he ran from the room, briefly stopping to show Belinda, Preet, and Ed the picture of Zac beaten to a pulp with a noose round his neck.

Belinda rushed forward and round to Karen's side of the desk. Karen was in a state of complete hysteria. Tugging at her hair, sobbing, and slapping the desk. She was losing the plot, a tidal wave of emotions colliding inside her with no discernible way of controlling them.

"Karen, it's going to be okay. We are here for you." Belinda threw her arm round Karen and pulled her in for a hug. Officers stood in Karen's doorway with tear-stained faces. The image was horrific. The intention deliberate. Zac's captors wanted to provoke a reaction and needed Karen to know that they were in control.

Preet rushed round to the other side of the desk with some tissues, handing them to Karen. "I know it doesn't seem like it, but it is news of some sorts. We know he's alive. The high-tech team will tear that image apart to look for the digital footprint."

Karen closed her eyes. She knew Preet meant well, and yes, it was news. Zac was alive. But she couldn't wash that image from her mind. His face showed signs of being battered, bloodied, and bruised. It appeared as if someone had used it as a punchbag for nothing more than pure twisted enjoyment.

But it was the image of the noose round his neck and the excruciating pain on his face that haunted her the most. There was desperation and fear in his wide eyes.

Karen gasped as another thought entered her mind. That was only a picture of Zac. What if the next picture she received was a similar one of Jade? *Please, God, no... no... no.* Jade might be tough, but a beating like this was more than most people could survive. She rocked back and forth as her hands trembled. A sour taste lined her mouth as the room spun. As she sat there, they had her just where they wanted her... waiting in dread for what would come next.

16

Shield returned two hours later with Karen's phone. He stepped into her office to find her still sat at her desk, head in hands, a black coffee now cold, untouched. The strain of the situation was clear in her posture, the weight of worry and fear bearing down on her shoulders as she slumped forward with her elbows resting on the desk.

"Here's your phone. The digital team is doing what they can. There's no metadata on the image. The EXIF, the exchangeable image file format, has been deleted, so it doesn't provide us with geotag data to give the GPS coordinates of where the photo was taken. Clever bastards. Still, they might recover something. Apparently, it's to do with layers of the image, so there might be data within the layers."

Karen looked up, her eyes red-rimmed and exhausted. The news about the lack of metadata was disheartening, but she clung to the sliver of hope that the digital team might still uncover something that could lead them to Zac.

Shield's brow furrowed as he took in Karen's appearance. "You look like shit. You look crap. Get some food inside you and then have a lie down. At this rate you're going to make yourself ill."

Karen huffed. "You know how to make a woman feel good. Did they teach you anything else in charm school?" she remarked.

"Loads more, but I'll save that for another day. I need to get back."

Karen watched as Shield marched out of her office, his broad shoulders disappearing through the doorway. It had taken her an hour to calm down after seeing Zac's picture. The image burnt into her mind, haunting her every thought. Belinda kept popping in to check up on her, a gentle presence amidst the chaos, but even her kindness couldn't ease the ache in Karen's heart.

The last few hours had been a rollercoaster, which left her more exhausted than ever. Each time she cried, it took a bit more out of her, the tears flowing freely as she grappled with the fear and uncertainty of Zac's fate. She wondered if the tears would ever stop or dry up, if the pain would ever ease.

Picking up her phone, she dialled Summer's number. A further risk review of Summer and Michelle had determined the need for them to be moved under armed guard to police safe housing. Karen imagined that the news hadn't gone down well with Michelle, and probably with Summer, either. But it was a decision taken by the chief constable following discussions with Detective Superintendent Kelly. He took the decision to move them to a safe house and emphasised the severity of the situation and the danger that these men posed.

"Hey, you, how are you holding up?" Karen asked when Summer answered, "I know it's late, but I wanted to make sure you're okay."

It was a few seconds before Summer replied. Her voice was soft and muffled as if she had been crying. "I'm scared, Karen. I want my dad back. Where is he?"

Karen gritted her teeth and fought back the anguish. She wanted to be there for Summer, to wrap her in a hug and promise her that everything would be alright. But she knew she couldn't make such promises, not when Zac's life hung in the balance. "We're doing everything we can to get your dad back. We have hundreds of officers out there now searching for him. I want him back too. You need to know, I will stop at nothing to make that happen."

Summer sobbed as she tried to say something, but it made little sense, and Karen didn't want to push. She could only imagine Summer's fear and confusion.

"Hey, listen. You're not alone. I'm here for you. Your dad's the number-one priority of every officer available. We'll do our best to find him, so you'd better be ready with the biggest hug you've ever given him."

"Yeah," Summer replied.

It tore Karen's heart to hear Summer like this. She didn't sound like a teenager, but more like a six-year-old.

"Do you... do you think it's the same people who took my friend? If they've taken Dad, they might take me?"

"No... No. Shush. No one is going to take you. There are four police officers at the house with you. They are big and ugly and it's going to take an awful lot to get past them. And there are more than a dozen close by. You are better protected than the Crown Jewels in the Tower of London," Karen reassured her, trying to inject humour into the situation.

"When will I see you, Karen?"

"Soon. I promise. Is your mum okay?"

"Yeah, sort of. She is mad at being told what to do."

"It's for her safety as well. We just need to get through

this and then we can get on with our lives again. Besides, we've got our Florida holiday to look forward to. I'm not going all that way without you. You are going to be my ride buddy, and we are going to eat Cinnabon's and drink frozen Butterbeer in the Wizarding World of Harry Potter until it's coming out of our ears."

"Don't forget the shopping in the Premium Outlets."

"How could I? We can shop to our heart's content. I haven't told your dad about that," Karen laughed.

Summer laughed back. And it was great to hear the lightness in her voice.

"I've got to go now, but you be brave and strong for me, okay? And I'll see you soon. Get some sleep."

"Okay. Night. Please bring Dad home."

"I promise. Love you."

"Love you, too."

Karen hung up, feeling so much better for making a call. It didn't feel good to make a promise she couldn't keep, but she needed Summer to carry hope to get through this. Karen rose from her chair and headed to the spare bedrooms on the ground floor. She needed a shower, a change of clothes, and a moment to herself to gather her thoughts and steel her resolve.

As the hot water cascaded over her, washing away the grime and sweat of the day, Karen let herself cry, great heaving sobs that wracked her body and left her gasping for air as she slid down the tiles and slumped to the shower tray. She cried for Zac, for Summer, for the life they had built together that now hung in the balance. She cried for the fear and uncertainty that gripped her heart, the knowledge that even with all her training and experience, she was powerless to bring Zac home.

But as the tears subsided, and the steam swirled round her, Karen felt a flicker of determination spark to life in her chest. Zac and Jade would be back, no matter what it took. She would bring Zac home to Summer, to the life they had looked forward to. And she would make sure the bastards who had taken them paid for what they had done.

17

Karen's eyelids grew heavy, fatigue finally claiming her after endless hours of worry over Zac's abduction. As she drifted into a restless sleep, the shadows in the room seemed to shift and dance round her, making her feel like she was floating.

I stand in the middle of a forest, trees in all directions pinning me in like a caged animal, the air thick with a sense of dread. A scuffling sound echoes from up ahead, followed by a muffled cry that sends a chill down my spine—it's Zac's voice. I break into a sprint, pushing past the low-hanging branches that whip and sting my face, my heart pounding with each step.

I enter a murky and cold clearing, and I'm met with a haunting sight. Zac is being dragged away by the group of armed, masked men. Their hold on him is unyielding, and Zac's struggles are futile against their combined strength. His eyes lock with mine, wide with terror, as he cries out my name.

"Karen! Help me. Please!" His voice cracks with desperation, the pleas piercing straight through me.

I race forward, driven on by a frantic need to reach him.

But the ground seems to stretch endlessly, and the faster I run, the further away Zac becomes, his figure growing smaller and smaller in the distance.

Panic rises in my chest as I push harder to reach him. My lungs burn with exertion. The rough ground tears shreds from the soles of my bare feet, but I hardly register the pain. All that matters is closing the gap and saving Zac from his captors.

Finally, there's a glimmer of hope. I'm within reach, my fingers extending towards his outstretched hand. For a fleeting moment, our fingertips brush, a tenuous connection forged. But then, a swirling vortex of inky blackness engulfs Zac, his anguished cries fading into an eerie silence.

He's gone. I stumble forward, my knees buckling, as I grasp at the air where he once was. "Zac!" I scream, my voice echoes in the emptiness.

Darkness presses in from all sides, suffocating me. I spin round, searching for any sign of him, but there's nothing but the oppressive shadows.

With a violent jolt, Karen bolted upright in bed, a scream ripping from her throat. "Zac!"

She gasped for air; her heart thundered in her chest. Beads of sweat trickled down her forehead and cheeks, her damp hair clinging to her face. Overwhelmed by a sense of confusion and disorientation, Karen gripped the covers and tried to separate the vivid nightmare from reality.

The atmosphere in the room was oppressive, with the shadows casting a menacing presence from all sides. Karen's eyes darted back and forth as she searched for any trace of Zac, but he was nowhere to be found. The echoes of his desperate pleas still rung in her ears and left her shaken to her core and utterly alone in the darkness.

She fumbled for her phone in the dark and tapped the screen. It was a little after four a.m. in the morning. A small window high on the wall confirmed the darkness outside as she got out of bed and headed for the shower. She was in no hurry to leave, the sound of running water a helpful distraction from the turmoil and chaos in her mind. Tears mixed with the water as it ran down her face. Her chest heaved as she cried. *When would this stop?* she questioned. The sense of loneliness and isolation had never been so overwhelming.

AN HOUR LATER, Karen returned to her office with a strong black coffee in hand. It still wasn't six a.m. but the SCU was busy. Her officers were pulling all-nighters to find their colleagues. She had never experienced such a deep sense of pride in being part of the police family. They were all going above and beyond of what was expected of them. And yet everything felt like such a mess. Just when everything was so good.

Her mind tracked back to Christmas Day. She had never felt so excited about Christmas. Even as a child, she'd felt that Christmas was overshadowed by the sadness of not being able to share it with her sister, Jane. Her parents had always made an effort to ensure Christmas was a cheerful event, but there was always a sense of something missing.

By comparison, Christmas at Zac's was incredible. Summer had screamed down the house in excitement as she'd hammered on their bedroom door before racing downstairs to lay out the Christmas presents in three piles, one for each of them. The three of them had sat on the floor in their pyjamas, each taking it in turn to open their presents. Zac was delighted with the three Ralph Lauren tops Karen and Summer had bought for him, as well as the Boss aftershave, and the joke present of a green mankini.

Summer had loved her new fluffy pyjamas, a few sweatshirts, and a top, all from PrettyLittleThing. Karen had felt a deep warmth when Summer had jumped up and thrown herself upon Karen and Zac, thanking them.

The joy continued as Karen had opened presents from Summer and Zac. Perfume, leather jacket, and a generous voucher to buy some new leather boots. Zac had bought her some saucy underwear to embarrass her, and she had felt her face flush upon opening the present. Summer had thrown a hand over her eyes in disgust, shouting "ew!"

Happy memories of family life, which were no doubt reflected millions of times up and down the country. Karen took a sip from her coffee. With everything that had happened in the last few days, Christmas felt like it was months ago.

Anita appeared in the doorway carrying her phone in one hand, and an insulated silver mug in the other. "Hi, Karen. I didn't know if you'd be here, but thought I would check. Are you okay? You look exhausted. Have you slept?"

Karen nodded. "I did, a few hours. It didn't help. But I'm holding up."

Anita stepped over to Karen's desk and rested her mug on the table before fishing something out of her back pocket. "Here you go. I got these for you. High energy and protein bars. You need to keep your strength up. And don't tell me you're not hungry, because I won't leave this room until you've had something to eat."

Karen smiled. "Thank you. That's kind of you." She picked up the Grenade bar, recognising them as the ones that Dan was always munching on. "Do you know, it's times like this that I wonder if the job is worth it. There's only so much we can cope with, given that it destroys marriages, harms lives, and drives people to drink, drugs, and worse."

"I know. It takes a certain person to do this job. Yes, it's shit, and a thankless task more often than not. Despite being limited by rules and regulations, we are able to make a difference. What's happening now is something so rare that none of us have experienced anything like this before. It's enough to break most people but I know you, Karen, you are strong and fierce."

Karen shrugged. "I don't feel like that at the moment."

"Understandable. But I think I know you well enough now. You'll let no one get the better of you and you will always fight until your last breath. That's what I admire about you. And at this difficult time, you need to draw on every ounce of your amazing strength to stay positive, hopeful, and not give up."

"Yes, Mum." Karen nodded.

"Right, enough of our cosy pillow talk. Let's put our war faces on and fight through another day. Call me if you need me." Anita grabbed her mug and gave Karen a wink before leaving.

Karen thanked the universe for bringing such amazing people like Anita into her life.

18

THE MAN'S eyes flickered open, his gaze fixed on the cold, hard ground beneath his bare feet. Time seemed to have lost all meaning in this dark, damp place. How long had it been since he had been brought here, days or just hours? Left alone, half-dressed, and hungry, he had long abandoned his efforts to grasp the fate that awaited him at the hands of his captors. Apart from offering a few sips of water, they left him alone.

Each time they came to check on him, their footsteps echoed off the walls, the sound reverberating through his bones. Cold seeped into his body, leaving his fingers and toes numb. They had beaten him once, a brutal, merciless assault which left him battered and broken. And then, they'd left him there, never uttering a word, never interrogating him, never even asking his name. His pleas for help and mercy went unheard, his cries echoing in the darkness, unanswered.

Dehydration left him confused, weak, and lightheaded. The constant darkness offered no clues whether it was day or night, no hint of the world that lay beyond.

He had lost all sense of time and place, his mind lost in a sea of despair and fear.

A noise pierced the silence, faint at first but growing louder with each passing second. Footsteps. Many footsteps. They were coming for him, their approach announced by the dreaded sound of their boots on the hard floor. He strained to see beyond the darkness, his eyes widening in fear as he tried to make out the shapes of his captors.

At first, there was only stillness, the blackness seeming to swallow all light and movement. But then, the shadows moved, a mass of silhouettes emerging from the gloom, advancing towards him with purposeful strides. His chest tightened, his heart pounding against his ribs as he struggled to breathe, the air rasping through his cracked and parched lips.

Why was he here? What did they have in store for him? Was this it? Was he about to take his last breath? The questions raced through his mind, each one more terrifying than the last.

The largest shadow detached itself from the congregation of silhouettes, its looming height becoming clear as it drew closer. As the figure approached, the man could make out more of his captor's features, the dim light casting an eerie glow on the man's face. In contrast to the others, who always concealed their faces behind balaclavas, this man made no attempt to hide his identity. His face was ugly, cold, and menacing.

The captor leaned in, his face inches away, his icy stare devoid of any hint of emotion or compassion. The man could feel the captor's breath on his skin, the stench of cigarettes and stale sweat filling his nostrils. He wanted to turn away, to close his eyes and shut out the horror of his situation, but he found himself transfixed, unable to look away from those piercing, merciless eyes.

"Please! Please don't hurt me. I don't know what you want with me. If it's money, I don't have any," the man begged, his voice hoarse and trembling. But his words fell on deaf ears. His captor remained silent, his expression unchanging. The other figures emerged from the darkness, forming a ring of menace round him, their eyes boring into him through the slits in their balaclavas.

The man's body shook, wracked by a mix of cold and fear. He looked at each captor, searching for a flicker of compassion, a hint of humanity in their eyes. But there was none to be found, only a chilling emptiness as if each had risen from the grave as demons of the devil.

Moments later, the main captor stepped forward, glancing over his shoulder into the darkness behind him. The man tried to follow his gaze, straining to see who or what the captor was looking at, but he could see nothing but an impenetrable wall of black. The captor nodded, as if receiving some unspoken command, before turning his attention back to the man. With a fluid, almost casual motion, he pulled a knife from his waistband, the blade glinting in the dim light as he closed the distance between them.

In that moment, the man knew with a sickening certainty that his life was about to end. This dank, cold cave would be where he took his last breath. He wanted to scream, to beg for mercy, to plead for his life, but the words stuck in his throat, choked off by the terror that consumed him.

A blood-curdling scream tore through the cave, the sound echoing off the stone walls, reverberating through the darkness. It only took a moment for the man to realise that the scream came from his own throat, ripped from the depths of his being by the sheer, primal terror that seized him. And then, as suddenly as it had begun, the scream abruptly stopped, replaced by a deafening silence that seemed to stretch on for an eternity.

In those final, horrifying moments, the man's life flashed before his eyes, a kaleidoscope of memories and regrets, of loves lost and dreams unfulfilled. He thought of his family, his friends, of all the things he had left unsaid and undone. And as the knife pierced his flesh and the searing pain consumed him, he experienced a strange sense of peace. He accepted the fate that had been dealt to him.

As he slipped into the darkness, his last thoughts were of the sad life he had lived, of the poor choices he had made that had brought him to this moment. And then, there was nothing but silence, a final, eternal silence that marked the end of his existence.

19

Shield was back in Karen's office late morning and showed little in the way of enthusiasm or encouragement as he stopped on the other side of the desk.

"Anything?" Karen asked.

Shield grimaced.

"I can't sit here like this any more. I feel like I'm in a goldfish bowl." Karen pointed to the glass wall that looked on to the hallway beyond. "Everyone gawps as they pass."

"I guess. Anyway, the super and CC have called in added help from the NCA. You and I are meeting the director of intelligence in the meeting room in five. Tidy yourself, you look like a sack of shit. Let's go."

Karen pulled a face and pursed her lips. Shield could be an obnoxious git. But she could cope with that. It was the arrival of the NCA at the station that troubled her more. She grabbed a brush from her drawer and ran it through her hair, the static crackling round her. Dressed in a pair of dark jeans and a Nike hoodie, it would have to do. After all, she was off duty.

The pair headed to the meeting room and entered to find Detective Superintendent Laura Kelly sitting across the table from a woman in a two-piece grey skirt suit. Beneath it was a white blouse, and she looked ever the consummate professional. Karen wasn't sure what to expect, but the woman looked young, with short brown hair styled in a pixie haircut. She stood up as Karen and Shield entered.

"Ah, Karen. There you are," Kelly announced. "I'd like to introduce you to Wendy Taylor, the director of intelligence at the NCA."

Wendy extended her hand, and Karen and Shield welcomed her before taking a seat at the table.

"Wendy is here to help us in our efforts to find Zac and Jade." Kelly turned towards Wendy. "Perhaps you could give my officers a quick rundown of your background."

Wendy nodded and smiled. "Of course. Thank you for taking the time to see me. I'm the director heading up the intelligence command, which consists of about two thousand officers deployed both here in the UK and internationally. I've been with the NCA for five years, and before that held senior roles within the Intelligence Corps in the British Army deploying operationally to Iraq and Afghanistan."

Wendy's credentials impressed Karen.

"Our job within my command is strategic intelligence assessment and to offer operational intelligence to identify and disrupt serious and organised crime. We've been working with other intelligence agencies on matters that concern your situation here." Wendy paused and took a moment to let that sink in with those round her.

Shield shifted in his chair. He looked bored more than anything else. But Karen was all ears.

"How is your work connected to the abduction of Zac and Jade?" Karen asked.

"We hold information that suggests Sally Connell may be responsible for starting this."

Karen slapped a hand on the table. "I knew this. I bloody knew she might be behind this. Her OCG was depleted before she left the country. How has she pulled this off?"

"To begin with, we had specific intelligence to suggest that Sally Connell would attempt to spring her brother from prison. He was due in court, but, following our advice, he appeared via a live video link from prison, and was then moved to a more secure unit. A prison within a prison."

Karen nodded and rubbed her forehead. The beginning of another headache loomed.

"Intelligence gathered by my unit indicated her presence in Morocco and later Germany, and through collaboration with Europol, we now believe that Sally Connell has forged a partnership with a Russian OCG in Frankfurt." Wendy took a photo from her folder and passed it round for the three officers to see.

Karen studied the image of a man triumphantly holding aloft an assault rifle. Cold eyes, and a weathered, unshaven face with cropped hair.

"This is Vitaly Andreev, aged fifty-four," Wendy continued, "the UK boss of the Kazanskaya crime group, from the region with the same name. He's been under surveillance since entering the UK illegally. We believe Sally Connell has instructed Andreev's men to carry out these abductions. In the span of the past twelve months, over thirty individuals connected to Andreev made their way into the country."

Karen narrowed her eyes and stared at Wendy. "If you know so much about them, why have we let them into the country?"

"We are playing the long game here. That many entering the country in such a short space of time suggested that something big was about to go down. Our European counterparts insisted we observed from a distance and feed intelligence back to them. There's a much wider operation happening on the continent, and they didn't want it being disrupted by events here." Wendy took the photo of Andreev and placed it back in her folder. "That is the least of our problems. Andreev's OCG is made up of numerous disgruntled Russian soldiers who spent the majority of their training and working life in the Russian mountains. They are used to tough conditions. His militia is dangerous and heavily armed."

"I don't like where this is going," Karen muttered as she looked at Kelly.

"Two weeks ago, Andreev and all the others that we were tracking disappeared."

Shield furrowed his brow. "What do you mean disappeared?"

"Exactly that. The phone conversations we were monitoring stopped. The places where we knew they were hiding lay empty, and our intelligence operatives on the ground couldn't find them. They just ghosted away."

Shield rested his elbows on the table and buried his head in his hands. "Shit. So you let them slip through your fingers," Shield growled.

"I wouldn't put it that way," Wendy barked back.

"Sounds like it to me," he added.

"So Andreev's men have abducted our officers...?"

Kelly asked for confirmation as she steered the conversation back on track.

"We believe so. Their trademark is abduction involving firearms. Back in Russia they were doing this a lot with politicians of influence and wealthy business owners, often abducting their families in return for huge ransoms, and the release of prisoners from Siberian jails. They live and operate in the hills making it almost impossible for the authorities to find them." Wendy tutted and rolled her eyes. "In fact, they are so dangerous that the authorities are too scared to go after them. Far too many were returning in body bags."

"Oh, Jesus. I appreciate what you're saying, but this isn't filling me with a lot of confidence." Karen sat back in her chair and stared at the ceiling.

"I appreciate that," Wendy replied. "Serious and organised crime is the most significant national security threat faced by the UK. Bribery, corruption, cyberattacks. It's all there. In the UK, we believe there are over fifty-thousand people with links to nearly five thousand OCGs. This figure is likely to be a conservative estimate. I'm just sorry that our work has crossed over in to the situation you find yourselves in."

Karen closed her eyes. "I can't get my head round this. A former London crime boss from an organisation that we dismantled is now in bed with one of the most dangerous OCGs to come out of Russia... Am I going mad here?"

"I'm afraid not, Karen." Wendy packed her files away and rose. "Unfortunately, I have to leave now. The heads of other intelligence partners and I have a meeting back in London. I'll feed back to you as soon as I know a bit more. My primary concern is finding out where Zac and Jade are being held." Wendy turned to Kelly. "Thank you for your time, detective superintendent. I'll see myself out."

Once Wendy left, Karen, Shield, and Kelly sat in silence. No one had anything to say as the enormity of their situation sunk in. They were now dealing with a group of individuals far more dangerous than any of them had seen before. This was far from being over.

20

KAREN RETURNED TO HER OFFICE, her mind in a whirlwind. A part of her refused to believe the truth of what she had heard from Wendy. She dropped into her chair and sat staring at the desk as her mind replayed the conversation. Time seemed to slow down.

How? How had it come to this? She squeezed her eyes shut and clenched her jaw.

The weight of the situation bore down on her like a heavy burden. She felt overwhelmed, unsure of how to process the news. Karen tried to take deep breaths, attempting to calm her racing thoughts, but the gravity of the situation made it nearly impossible.

Shock turned to anger. Sally Connell should have died beside her brother in a hail of bullets. The woman had got away with it and had now come back stronger than ever. They had to find a way of shutting her down, but judging from the intelligence revealed to them, the only way to do that would be to wipe out Connell and Andreev's gang. It would be a bloodbath and she didn't want the deaths of other officers on her conscience for evermore. The thought of more lives being lost in this battle against Connell and Andreev's gang made her stomach churn. She knew that as a police officer, she had sworn to protect and serve, but the potential cost of taking down this criminal organisation seemed too high.

This was out of her hands. Shield and Kelly were leading this, and she was nothing more than a bystander. With armed officers stationed in her building, patrolling the grounds, and on the main gate, it would be impossible for her to leave without being noticed. Besides, where would she go? What would she do single-handedly? She would play straight into Connell's hands.

Stress was taking its toll. The foggy head, irrational thoughts, mood swings, and frustration. To add to that, a lack of sleep, nightmares, and a loss of appetite. Karen had never felt so rough and there was no end in sight. Her heart ached for Zac and Jade. The two closest people to her who she dearly loved. Jade didn't deserve any of this, and Karen wondered how Jade could rebuild her life. The mental and emotional trauma would stay with her friend forever.

The first time in her life she had found true love and met the man of her dreams, and now feared for his safety. He was at the mercy of ruthless killers and as hard as she tried, the thought of never seeing him again haunted her.

The physical and emotional exhaustion was wearing Karen down. She rubbed her temples, trying to ease the tension headache that had been building. This was all her fault. Connell's thirst for vengeance and fury were directed at Karen and those closest to her. She had lost her criminal organisation, lost one brother, and seen the other banged up for a long time. Connell was mad and exacting revenge.

Karen was pulled away from her thoughts when

Belinda appeared in the doorway laden with a few sports bags.

"I'm not disturbing you, am I?"

"No, come in. It's not like I've got anything to do."

Belinda set down her bags by Karen's desk and grabbed a spare seat. "That's all your stuff in the bags you asked for. I also grabbed anything else that you might need like your hairdryer, straighteners, make-up, shoes, and another pair of trainers."

"Did you leave anything behind?" Karen smirked.

Belinda smiled.

"Thanks. I'm hoping I don't need most of this, but I only had a few items here, and I don't know how long this is going to..." Karen trailed off. She didn't want to go there and assume the worst. "How is it over there?"

Belinda raised a brow. "Locked down like an armed fortress. I know no one is in there, but judging by our heavy presence outside, you would think that the President of the United States had moved in."

"That's good. Zac needs a house to come home to. The last thing I need is Connell burning the place down."

"Are you hungry?"

Karen scrunched her nose. "Not really."

Belinda rose from her chair. "Well, I'm not having that. I picked up a seafood paella from Sainsbury's. It's big enough for two, so let me pop it in the microwave and I'll be back in ten minutes. You and I both need to eat, and I won't take no for an answer."

Karen smiled and nodded. She watched as Belinda scooted off, thinking how kind and generous that was of her. There were people all round her doing whatever they could to support her and lift her spirits. There was just as good a vibe here in York as there was in London. One which nurtured camaraderie, friendship, and a sense of belonging.

Belinda spent the next hour fussing over Karen, making sure she ate a proper meal and hydrated herself with water. They sat and talked, with Belinda doing her utmost to keep the conversation light and fun.

Not long after they'd finished and Belinda was gathering up the plates and empty water bottles, Karen's desk phone rang. It was her boss, Kelly, asking to see her in the Forensics Unit evidence room.

21

Karen walked over to the Forensics Unit, each step filled with a mixture of curiosity and trepidation. An uncomfortable knot of apprehension unfurled in the pit of her stomach, as she remembered the tone in her boss's voice during the quick call, which was laced with an undercurrent of tension.

As she approached the closed door, she sensed the gravity of the situation, like a physical weight pressing down upon her. Her whole body felt heavy and sluggish. Could she handle any more bad news? The hallway seemed to stretch on, each step becoming more difficult than the last. The silence was oppressive, broken only by the pounding of her own heart in her ears.

Kelly wasn't alone—the muted voices from within revealed DCI Shield, the assistant chief constable, and Bart, the crime scene manager. The fact they had been called in told Karen that whatever awaited her was serious. Her hands felt clammy as she wiped them on her jeans.

Karen paused outside the door, her hand resting on

the handle. She took a deep breath, trying to steady her nerves, but the unease continued to churn in her gut. The presence of so many high-ranking officers only heightened her anxiety. She knocked on the door and turned the handle, stepping into the room, which though big, felt cramped and stuffed with so many bodies. The air was thick with solemnity, the faces of the officers reflecting the weight of the circumstances like a physical burden they all carried. Karen's gaze was drawn to the small cardboard package resting on a worktop to one side, its unassuming appearance belying the potential menace it contained.

Those present turned in unison to face Karen. She felt the knot tighten in her stomach.

"Someone delivered this for you an hour ago," Kelly began, her voice grave and measured, as if she had carefully chosen each word to limit its impact. "There was a delay in opening it because of the need to scan and check for noxious substances, given the current elevated threat level towards you, we needed to be sure it posed no risk to you, any other officer, and the station itself."

ACC Jackson took a step towards Karen and placed a hand on her arm. "It's not good, and you don't have to see it. It's your choice."

"What is it?" she asked.

Jackson glanced over his shoulder at the others before returning his attention to Karen. "It's a severed human body part. As yet we don't know who it belongs to, but the accompanying note says it may belong to Zac. We wanted to let you know, but I'd suggest that you don't see it."

Shock paralysed Karen as she swayed a little. The ACC's words hung in the air, a gentle warning that whatever lay within the package was not for the faint of heart. Karen appreciated the concern, but she knew she had to face whatever it was head-on. She couldn't hide from the truth, no matter how painful it might be. Karen nodded. "Thanks, but I have to do this."

"Very well." The ACC stepped back, clearing the way to the worktop.

Karen's heart pounded in her chest, the rapid staccato drumming reverberating in her ears as she moved closer, her eyes fixed on the innocuous-looking package that seemed to hold such ominous implications. A bead of sweat trickled down her back as she reached out with a trembling hand. As she lifted the flaps, Karen's hands shook, her fingers feeling numb and disconnected from her body. Time seemed to slow down, each second stretching out into an eternity. She braced herself for the worst, her mind conjuring up images of unspeakable horrors that might await her within the confines of the cardboard.

The sight that greeted her robbed her of breath, a visceral recoil seizing her body. Nestled inside the box, a severed human ear lay in a twisted, bloodied heap, the dried crimson staining the pale flesh like a grotesque mockery of life. Beside it, a scribbled note bore the chilling words: "A present from Zac."

Karen's world shattered in an instant, the grisly contents of the package searing themselves into her mind with a sickening clarity. She stumbled back, her hand flying to her mouth as a strangled cry tore from her throat. "Fuck no! Please, no," Karen muttered.

The room seemed to spin and tilt as the weight of the grisly discovery crashed over Karen like a tidal wave of epic proportions. Her stomach lurched, bile rising in her throat as she stumbled towards the rubbish bin by the door and retched as the contents of her recent paella spilled out in a bitter stream.

Gasping for air, she grabbed for the wall to steady

herself. Her vision blurred and swam, the edges of her sight growing hazy and indistinct. Her knees buckled, the world tilting at a sickening angle as the shock overwhelmed her senses. She crumpled to the floor, the thud of her body striking the cold floor.

Karen's body felt disconnected from her mind, her limbs heavy and unresponsive as she lay on the floor. The voices of the officers swirled round her, their words muffled and distant, as if spoken through a thick fog. She tried to focus on their faces, but they seemed to shift and waver, their features distorted by the haze of her fading consciousness.

She heard the muffled voices of the officers rushing towards her, their words fading into a distant hum as she was dragged under. Kelly's face swam into view for a moment, contorted with concern, before everything faded to black.

22

Voices. Muffled voices that faded in and out. It took a few moments for Karen to open her eyes, only to find herself lying on her side, her face pressed into the vinyl floor, the cold of the tiles in marked contrast to the heat in her cheeks which felt like raging furnaces.

"Keep taking slow and steady breaths," a voice instructed.

Shoes. That's all her eyes focused on. Several pairs of shoes crowded round her. She opened and closed her eyes and licked her dry lips. What had just happened? Her brain wouldn't engage.

"How are you feeling now?" the voice asked.

It took every ounce of effort for Karen to crane her head just a few inches to see a woman kneeling beside her, a soft smile on her face.

"Who...? You?"

"I'm Samantha, a first-aider. You've had a bit of a turn and fainted."

"Where... am I?" Karen closed her eyes for a second.

She felt clammy and sick. Her fringe clung to her damp forehead.

Kelly leaned forward to get closer to Karen. "You are in the Forensics Unit, Karen. You had a bit of a shock. Are you well enough to sit up?"

Karen nodded. Between Samantha, Bart, and DCI Shield, they helped her to her feet and placed her in one of the comfy visitor chairs before Samantha offered her a glass of water. Karen took a few sips to ease the harshness in her throat. It was all coming back to her. Kelly's call, the reception party, the box! She glanced over at the worktop. It was gone.

Despite feeling groggy and disoriented, Karen had no choice but to confront the haunting reality that Zac's captors had escalated their torment. They delivered a sickening message that would forever be seared into her memory, serving as a grim reminder of the depths of depravity to which they were willing to sink.

"Where is it?"

"One of Bart's team has taken it away," Kelly replied.

"That can't be his. Please, it can't be his." Karen sniffed as she wiped her moist eyes with the back of her hands. An icy chill ran through her body that made her shiver. For a fleeting moment, she imagined Connell sending Zac back in pieces as the ultimate act of torment and revenge.

"That's what we need to find out. A courier delivered it. They didn't hang round to give any details, but we are analysing footage from the front desk to build a composite of the rider. I'm sorry you had to see that."

"It's okay, ma'am. A part of me didn't want to, but curiosity and the need to know got the better of me. It must be a joke. They wouldn't do that, would they?"

DCI Shield folded his arms across his chest. "I know you don't want to hear this, but I wouldn't put anything past them. They are ruthless and dangerous. Don't forget, the regions these guys come from don't have the security or emergency services in place like we do. It's lawless. Many of the police are corrupt, and killings are frequent and violent."

Karen wondered if Shield possessed any filter when he spoke. It wasn't what she wanted to hear, and whether or not it was deliberate on Shield's part, it did little to relieve the knot of anxiety that twisted her insides.

"Have we had any news on Jade? A note? Video? Anything to confirm she's alive?" Karen said, turning towards Kelly.

"Nothing as yet. We don't have any promising leads yet to indicate where they might be held. I'm hoping they're close by, but they could be anywhere. Considering Sally Connell's old stomping ground is London, there's always a risk that they've been taken there. Connell would like that. It would be a clear message to her rivals that she was back, and she meant business."

"Do you want me to speak to my old bosses in London?" Karen asked.

Kelly raised a hand. "ACC Jackson has already spoken with the commissioner. They are doing everything they can to find Connell's current location. I've spoken with Wendy at the NCA. Following this development and with the help of other intelligence services, they are doing a deep trawl of all communications looking for any keywords such as York, police, courier, you, Zac, or Jade. They are actively searching for anything like that which may be linked to us."

"Do you really think that's going to help?" Karen questioned.

"Do you have a better idea?" Shield snapped.

Karen lowered her head. She didn't. Shield and Kelly

were doing their best, and with the assistance of the NCA and other intelligence partners, there was little more they could do. Connell and Andreev's men were running this. As yet, there was no one else in the frame, not even the Harmans. This was bigger than anything she had dealt with, and though Karen had put away hundreds of people in her career, she could count on one finger the number of people who would have the connections, muscle, money, and bollocks to do something like this.

If, as they suspected, it was Sally Connell and Andreev's OCG, they were dealing with a hardened group of individuals who had been involved in a scale of violence never seen before in this country.

23

Karen threw the skin of a banana in the bin beside her desk. Enjoying seafood paella had been short-lived, and as Karen recalled the incident in the Forensics Unit, she felt annoyed and embarrassed by what had happened. Of all people, throwing up and passing out in front of the ACC ranked up there as one of the most embarrassing moments in her career.

She grabbed her phone and dialled Bart.

"Hey, Karen. I know what you're going to say, but it's going to take time to do the DNA analysis on the ear."

Just the mention was enough to make her feel uneasy as the image flashed through her mind. "No, not that. I was curious if your team had obtained any evidence from the burnt-out vehicles?"

"Oh, right. One second. Let me check."

Karen heard Bart tap away on his keyboard.

"Right, here it is. As yet we've not been able to recover anything of interest. It was a clean job. The fire was so intense that the framework of the vehicles buckled under the intensity of the heat. They did a proper number on them."

Karen guessed that would be the case. She doubted the old Molotov cocktail approach would suffice.

"They used petrol as the accelerant. Springs from the seats were all that remained inside."

"Are your team still on it?"

"Yes. I doubt they will find anything. We recovered the VIN plates and engine numbers and passed them on to DCI Shield's team. We've also completed the fibre analysis from samples recovered from both Zac's house and Jade's apartment. Nothing startling there either. Black polycotton fibres. Usual composition."

Belinda appeared in Karen's doorway. Karen waved her in and told her to take a seat while she listened to Bart. Karen felt the frustration boil within her listening to the feedback. There was nothing there. Absolutely nothing. She zoned out for a few moments. Everything that Karen had heard so far about this case confirmed in her mind that Sally Connell was behind this or involved in some way. The problem was there was no CCTV evidence, no sightings, and no call data or traffic to confirm this. It was the assumption that DCI Shield and Kelly were working on, but deep down, Karen knew. Connell was smart, but she had come back to the UK as a force to be reckoned with.

Ending the call, she placed the phone on a desk and stared at Belinda. "Bel, I can't take much more of this. I'm losing my mind and I'm struggling to keep it together. This is hard on me. I'll give as good as it takes, but this has broken me."

"I know, Karen. We are all finding it hard, so I can't imagine the effect it's having on you. You have to stay hopeful. It's the only way to get through this. We'll get them back, I know it."

Karen hoped that too, but a part of her dreaded the possibility whether they would come back dead or alive.

"In the absence of DCI Shield, I thought I'd update you on some tasks the team is doing. I along with a few others have been doing a deep trawl of CCTV footage recovered from Zac's house. It's clear that the abduction was being planned for days and maybe even weeks. We found three occasions in the seven days prior to Zac's abduction when the same vehicle cruised past between one a.m. and three a.m. We believe it's a black Mercedes. The plates were false."

"I'm not surprised. This was planned to the finest detail. If it's Andreev's men, many of them are ex-military, it would have been part of their reconnaissance experience."

Bel agreed. "On each occasion they stopped for a second or two before driving away. We also found clips of two men walking past and slowing when they reached his front garden. They looked at their phones and then looked round before walking off again. They were scoping the area and his home."

"What time were those events recorded?"

Bel checked her notes. "The first sighting was at twelve forty-three a.m., the second was at two seventeen a.m."

"Zac had no chance."

"I know, Karen. That's all I've got at the moment," Bell said. She rose from her chair. "Is there anything I can get you?"

"No. It's fine, thanks. I really appreciate everything you've done. Not just on the job front, but..." Karen tipped her head to one side and shrugged, "well, you know... caring."

Bel smiled. "I expect a glowing review during my annual appraisal."

Karen smiled. Bless her. "Go on, get back to your job before DCI Shield wonders where you are."

Karen watched as Belinda disappeared. It was late in the evening. The day had flown by and though she wanted to stay up, scared she would miss any developments, she needed to rest. She rose from her chair and flicked off her office light before heading to her bedroom. She doubted if she could sleep, but perhaps she could rest her eyes in the darkness and soothe that gritty, dry sensation that had left them bloodshot.

24

Karen woke with a pained groan, feeling as though someone had battered and bruised her body. In part because of the lumpy mattress that offered little to no support for her back. Meant for a temporary one-night stay, it left her tight and sore. The past few nights had been a relentless blur, spent confined within the dreary, impersonal walls of the small bedroom at the police station. A makeshift refuge provided to offer safety but felt more like a prison cell closing in round her.

The dull, lifeless room had become her reluctant hideaway from the constant questions and awkward stares, and a desperate measure taken in the wake of the horrific "present" from Zac's captors. Karen shuddered as the memory resurfaced—the sickening sight of that severed ear, the scrawled handwritten taunt accompanying it. Even now, she could taste the bitter bile that had risen in her throat and scorched her taste buds.

As she peeled herself from the scratchy sheets, a dull ache pulsed through her muscles, a constant reminder of the restless night spent awake staring into the darkness. Her mind was a fog of fragmented thoughts and half-formed nightmares, each more disturbing than the last, which left her heart thumping with a tightness in her throat.

Karen's thoughts drifted to her boss, Kelly, whose overbearing protectiveness had become more like a stranglehold than a security measure. The woman's absolute refusal to allow her even a momentary reprieve from the station's confines, even with an armed escort, was suffocating. She was desperate to see Summer, but knew Kelly meant well, but Karen had never been one to conform or stick to orders. Karen could almost picture the disapproving scowl and bollocking, the icy stare, and the lectures about needing to stick to safety protocols. It made her grind her teeth with frustration.

Enough was enough. A renewed sense of determination surged through Karen as she stepped in to the shower, the warm water rinsing away the remnants of her restless night and awakening her senses. She couldn't stay holed up like this, not when Zac and Jade's lives hung in the balance, a ticking clock counting down to an unthinkable outcome which she forced to the back of her mind.

Invigorated, Karen towelled off and threw on a tracksuit, not caring what others thought. She tied her hair into a high ponytail and checked herself in the mirror one last time. Karen decided she was done playing by Kelly's rules, done sitting idly by while her loved ones suffered at the hands of their sick and twisted captors.

With steely determination, she strode down the corridor, her footsteps echoing with conviction. She didn't care about protocols or chain of command—not any more. This was personal, and she would tear down any obstacle standing in her way.

Karen didn't bother knocking as she reached DCI Shield's office, pushing through the door with a force that made it slam against the wall.

"I want in on the investigation," she said with no nicety, her voice carrying the weight of her unwavering determination.

Shield's brow furrowed, his expression a mixture of concern and exasperation as he met her fiery gaze. "You're too emotionally involved, Karen. You can't remain objective in a case like this. And besides, I don't want my arse kicked out of the force for disobeying orders."

Karen rested her hands on her hips. "Objectivity went out of the window when they sent me that bloody ear," she replied, her tone laced with a flash of anger. The words hung in the air, a visceral reminder of the depravity they were up against. "I need to find Zac and Jade before it's too late. Before those sick bastards take this any further and send me more body parts. Jade won't be handling this too well. We need to find them now!"

Shield pinched the bridge of his nose, letting out a weary sigh as he leaned back in his chair. "Kelly will have my head if I bring you in on this, you know that. You're breaking every rule in the book and skinning my fat, lardy arse at the same time."

"I don't care what Kelly says and your arse isn't my problem. You're big and ugly enough to stick up for yourself," Karen snapped, her hands balling into fists at her sides.

"Looks like you didn't go to charm school either!"

"I'm done sitting on the sidelines, watching from behind the bloody glass walls of my office while those bastards torment me."

The air crackled with tension as they locked eyes, two

unyielding forces colliding in a battle of wills. Shield relented, his shoulders sagging in resignation.

"Shit. Fine," he grumbled, pushing himself to his feet. "Jesus, you've got some shiny brass balls. But you play by my rules, understood? No cowboy stunts, no running off half-cocked. We do this my way, or you're out, and I'll drag you to the gates myself. Got it?"

Karen gave a curt nod, her jaw clenched. She would agree to his terms, for now. But she knew in her heart that she would stop at nothing to bring Zac and Jade home safely—even if it meant defying orders and putting her own life on the line.

"I received a lead this morning," Shield continued, his tone all business as he grabbed his jacket from the back of the chair. "A Russian gang member linked to Andreev's outfit is under investigation by the NCA for the abductions. He's banged up in Wakefield."

Karen felt a spark of hope flicker within her. A lead, yes.

"Let's go," Shield said, heading for the door. "We won't find them doing a merry dance here."

Without a word, Karen fell in step beside him, her determination unwavering. A rush of excitement filled her with hope and a sense of purpose. They needed to confront this Russian gang member, prise the truth from him by whatever means necessary. And if he refused to cooperate... well, then, his stay in prison would be a painful one.

Karen's willingness to just fall in line had shattered long ago. She would do whatever it took to save Zac and Jade, even if it meant bending the rules again like she'd done occasionally in her career. After all, she mused as they strode down the corridor, she had already received her baptism into that bleak world when that bloodstained box had arrived.

There was no going back now. Not until Zac and Jade were safe, warm in her embrace once more.

25

KAREN SAT in tense silence for the entire journey to Wakefield, her hands tucked under her thighs, and her gaze fixed out of her window as the countryside rolled by in a blur of muted greens and browns. Arguing with DCI Shield seemed to have strengthened their tenuous relationship in a strange, unspoken way. Perhaps he simply wasn't used to others standing up to his gruff authority, and for that small show of backbone, he had begrudgingly accepted her as something akin to an equal.

She'd always harboured a dislike for the man, a resentment that had simmered from the moment they'd first crossed paths in the middle of a field. Shield's arrogant swagger, his argumentative nature, and blunt delivery had rubbed Karen the wrong way. And those traits hadn't faded with time—if anything, they'd become worse according to officers who worked beside him.

Yet, as much as she resented Shield's brash demeanour and insistence on ripping into anyone who dared question him, Karen couldn't deny his achievements. Shield's case clear-up and conviction rates were among the highest in the entire force, numbers he wasn't shy about flaunting at every opportunity. He did not try to mask his self-importance, taking a perverse pride in antagonising both criminals and colleagues alike with his callous one-liners and dismissive sneers.

By all accounts, they should have drummed DCI Shield out of the service years ago for his flagrant disregard of protocol and inability to play nicely with others. Karen sensed even Kelly trod carefully round him. And yet, he remained—an ill-tempered, foul-mouthed pain in the arse that the force tolerated.

As they pulled up to the imposing walls of Wakefield prison, Karen felt a simmering flame of determination reignite deep within her core. This was it—their first legitimate lead in far too long, a crack that could shed light on Zac and Jade's whereabouts. She would do whatever it took to extract answers, consequences be damned.

After passing through the checkpoints and signing in as visitors, a prison officer ushered them into an interrogation room—a painfully drab space consisting of only a battered table, four mismatched chairs bolted to the floor, and a CCTV camera mounted high on the wall. The blinking red light of the camera confirmed that their actions were being monitored and recorded.

"Victor Grozev, aged thirty-seven," Shield began, his gruff voice holding no trace of warmth as they settled in to wait. "One of Andreev's foot soldiers, serving twenty-eight years for firearms trafficking, drug offences, and shooting a rival through the eye at point-blank range."

Karen nodded curtly, her jaw clenching as she filed away the unsavoury details. She saw this meeting as a turning point—their chance to finally unravel the thread and discover what depraved minds were truly behind Zac and Jade's abductions before their trail went stone-cold.

The heavy door creaked open, and a hulking prison guard entered flanking a man who could only be Victor Grozev. He had a thick frame with wiry muscle, and his shoulders strained against the fabric of the grey tracksuit as the prison guard led him to the chair across from them. Grozev's gaze was wary and distrustful as he studied them, upper lip curling in a faint snarl.

The interview began in earnest with Shield asking questions about where the officers were being held, and where was Andreev, but it soon became clear that their guest was in no mood to cooperate. Grozev deflected every question with a stony silence or a vulgar reply in thickly accented English, his expression an impenetrable mask of disdain.

After several fruitless minutes of Karen and Shield losing their composure, Shield nodded towards the camera mounted overhead. Her brow furrowed in confusion for just a moment before realisation struck—in the next instant, the telltale red blink of the camera stopped.

Before Karen could so much as part her lips to say anything, Shield jumped to his feet and lunged across the table in a blur of motion. His meaty hands shot out, gripping Grozev by the ears and slamming the man's face down on to the battered steel surface with a nauseating crunch.

A guttural howl of agony split the air as Grozev's nose exploded in a fountain of crimson. Karen recoiled in shock and revulsion, her heart stuttering as she watched the scene unfold. Shield didn't stop there and did it again with even more force the second time.

"I want answers, you Russian bastard," Shield snarled, his fingers tangled in Grozev's greasy hair as he wrenched the man's head back with vicious force. Flecks of blood spattered across his contorted features and more dripped down his front and on to the table. "And you're going to give them to me, one way or another, even if I have to cut off your bollocks."

Grozev responded by spitting a thick gobbet of blood and phlegm on to the floor, his narrowed eyes burning with defiant hatred. "Go to hell, pig."

Shield's knuckles showed bone-white, tendons straining against the skin, ready to attack for a third time. "Listen closely, you piece of shit," he hissed through gritted teeth. "The minute we find our officers alive and well, I'll have you on the first flight out of this shithole, headed straight back to your precious Russia."

Leaning in until his face was mere inches from the battered prisoner, Shield's voice took on a dangerous purr. "I may not have the best grasp of your gutter language, but I promise you this—*trakhnut yego devushku* as soon as you get home."

Despite the pain and humiliation he'd just endured, a toothy smile spread across Grozev's bloodied face, revealing nicotine-stained teeth.

"I'll give you one hour to reconsider my offer before I withdraw it," Shield said after a tense pause, straightening and smoothing the creases from his jacket. "Think carefully about your next move, because it might be your last. There are some influential people I know in here, and I have a few favours owed to me."

Shield rose and banged on the door. With a curt nod to the guards, Grozev was hauled away, leaving a trail of smeared blood droplets in his wake. Karen could only gaze at Shield, her expression caught somewhere between abject shock and a grudging admiration for his brutal pragmatism.

"Interesting... interrogation technique. They never taught us that one at Hendon," she managed at last once the ringing in her ears had faded enough to allow her to speak.

"Worth a try," Shield grunted in response, straightening his tie as they made their way out to the car. "But their code runs tighter than a nun's crutch or a duck's arse."

Karen raised a brow as she shook her head, reality settling in with all the weight of a sledgehammer's blow. The righteous lines between defensive and offensive action had blurred into one as they tossed aside the rules and protocols governing their conduct.

"What did you say to him in Russian?"

It was a few moments before Shield replied with a smirk. "My Russian is shite, but I think I promised he could screw his girlfriend as soon as he got home."

Karen rolled her eyes. And as the prison walls disappeared behind them, Karen found herself at peace with Shield's behaviour, though she'd never tell him.

No price too high to pay, and no act too vicious if that's what it took to see her loved ones alive and whole once more.

26

KAREN TOOK a seat at the back of the briefing room. Shield stood at the front, the top button on his shirt undone with his tie loosened. He wasn't chronically overweight or anything like that, but he had a belly on him that left his shirt buttons straining. He had what Karen would call a dad bod, and with his hands tucked in his trouser pockets and his shoulders rounded and slumped forward, he fitted the bill.

The interview with Grozev replayed in her mind. She had always tried to conduct every interview professionally and legally, but Shield had just broken every rule. When he'd launched across the table and attacked Grozev, his actions had taken her by surprise. The thought of intervening had crossed her mind, but at this point, she was beyond caring and wanted answers regardless of how they were obtained. Shield hadn't uttered a word on the journey home, but she had noticed the white of his knuckles as he'd gripped the steering wheel.

Shield addressed the group of officers. "Okay, you lot. Listen up. Karen and I went to visit one of Andreev's associates. I hoped he would squeal and reveal what Andreev's group was up to, and perhaps where they were, but despite my best *persuasive* efforts, he kept his trap shut." Shield tutted. "I gave him an hour to consider my offer," Shield checked the clock on the wall behind him, "and considering our journey was just under an hour, I guess he wasn't in the mood to take me up on it."

The group of officers, which numbered fifty to sixty, listened in silence. Despite being January, it was warm and stuffy in the room, and it didn't help that the radiators were pumping out more heat to add to all the bodies crammed in.

"What have we got?" he asked.

Ed raised his hand. "Belinda and I scoured the local area for additional CCTV footage. We recovered a brief clip from a newsagent's a mile away from DCI Walker's home. We caught the white van and black Mercedes racing past at speed. It's only a second or two, but it helped us to build a better picture of the route they followed."

"Good. And what about at Jade's place?"

Belinda chipped in. "Again, we have been able to identify two separate occasions where a black Audi A6 and a blue Octavia were passing. They were the same vehicles spotted on CCTV footage less than a hundred yards from Jade's apartment. All four vehicles converged because we got an ANPR hit on the A1237 north of the city, and then they took the B1363 north. We are still looking for further footage to confirm where they went after that."

The news excited Karen. Piece by piece a picture was forming of the route the abductors took and where police resources needed to focus their investigation.

"Good work. I want the pair of you to organise extra resources to help you. You need to find every house, café, pub, B & B, and farm building along that road. Knock on every bloody door. We need every second of footage. Let's see how far they went."

Belinda and Ed nodded.

Ty spoke next. "Sir, we've made calls to all second-hand dealers in York. Unfortunately, we hit a brick wall. But we extended our search and ran further checks on the VIN plates from the burnt-out vehicles. The black Mercedes was purchased from a second-hand dealer in Norwich and the blue Octavia from a backstreet garage in Blackpool. The garage in Norwich didn't have any CCTV, but the one in Blackpool does. We'll be reviewing the footage straight after this meeting."

Shield nodded and tapped a finger on his chin. The black Mercedes was used in Zac's abduction, and the Octavia was used in Jade's. It was interesting to note that they had purchased both cars at different ends of the country, which confirmed the effort the gang had gone to in order to avoid suspicion.

Ty continued. "Three nights before Zac and Jade were abducted, someone stole the white Transit and black Audi A6. Both vehicles came from the Wakefield area."

Karen and Shield exchanged a glance. *Coincidence?* she wondered.

Shield continued with the briefing, closing off questions before sending his team on the way. As they left, Karen spotted Kelly coming in through a side door. She loitered inside and waited for the investigating team to leave so only Karen and Shield remained.

"Ma'am," Karen said.

Kelly nodded. "I'm glad I've got you both here. The DNA analysis on the ear has come back."

Karen's chest tightened, and her eyes widened, fearing the worst.

"It's good news. It doesn't belong to Zac... or Jade, for that matter. My guess is that someone sent it to you with the sole purpose of upsetting you."

"Bastards," Karen fumed as her jaw clenched. "Sorry, ma'am." Karen let out a few deep sighs as she brought her racing heart under control. "Who does it belong to then?"

Kelly shrugged. "We don't have a match on the DNA database, so we don't know yet."

Karen ran a hand through her hair and paced round the room. They were going round in circles.

"Karen, I sense your frustration. We are doing everything we can. We have a task force of over three hundred officers deployed in the search for Zac and Jade. I received a call from Wendy at the NCA moments ago. Wendy's team has been liaising with the intelligence services and called in a few favours with GCHQ. She confirmed the interception of chatter between key contacts within Andreev's OCG."

This was the news that Karen needed. She perked up as she returned to her spot near Kelly.

Kelly continued. "They managed to identify streams of communication being exchanged between several regions in Russia and Frankfurt... and the Yorkshire area."

Karen and Shield stared at each other in disbelief before returning their attention to Kelly.

Kelly nodded, a reassuring smile spreading across her face. "This is great news. Bloody brilliant. We have credible evidence to believe that Andreev's OCG is behind the abduction. It's their MO and we know they are on our patch."

Karen punched the air as she walked away, the excitement bubbling inside her. "Yes!"

"Have they picked up any communications involving Sally Connell?" Shield asked.

Karen spun round, desperate for the answer.

Kelly shook her head as she turned to leave, pausing at the door. "Nothing as yet. All the voices are male, and the dialect is Russian. I'm confident she's here, and she's being clever at staying under the radar to avoid drawing heat."

It was a point Karen agreed with. Connell had changed. She had gone from being the mouthpiece who wasn't afraid of a verbal duel with Karen, to lurking in the shadows and maintaining radio silence. To Karen it sounded like Sally Connell had taken on a more strategic role, which meant she kept her face out of the limelight.

"Thanks for the update, ma'am," both Shield and Karen replied in unison.

27

Jade's eyes snapped open, but the inky blackness enveloping her remained as impenetrable as ever. The coarse black fabric hood thrown over her head allowed no teasing sliver of light to pierce the disorienting void she found herself trapped in. A violent tremor wracked her slight body as a bone-deep chill cut through her—a cold so biting and relentless that it seemed to have taken up permanent residence within her, gnawing away at any lingering warmth like a ravenous beast.

Fatigue hung heavy in her bones, weighing her down. The dehydration and unrelenting fear had left Jade's mind foggy and numb, with thoughts slipping through her grasp like fistfuls of sand trickling from between splayed fingers.

The only thought she clung on to was why? Why was she here and what did they have planned for her?

All she knew with any certainty was the endless cycle of darkness, thirst, men lurking close to her, and a steadily encroaching chill that hit her every night.

Jade strained to listen. The only sounds which

reached her with any certainty were the faint drips and subterranean groans from her surroundings—the echoing plinks of water, coupled with occasional distant shuffles and muted murmurs from her unseen captors.

Those voices were little more than indistinct rumbles that made no sense to her. Low, gravelly tones that could have belonged to any number of men, uttered in a language Jade couldn't understand. She focused every iota of her flagging concentration to decipher their words, but without luck.

A sudden eruption of raucous laughter caused her to flinch. Were they laughing at her? Finding perverse amusement in her desperate plight? Mocking the hopes of rescue she still desperately clung to?

Jade pulled her legs tighter into the chair, hoping they wouldn't decide to turn their amusement upon her. She'd survived so far without them laying a finger on her. So many thoughts had crossed her mind, fully expecting some of them to be enacted on her, but she'd been lucky. No beatings or sexual intent. She prayed it would remain that way, and so far, her captors seemed content to leave her in relative peace and allow the psychological torments of sensory deprivation and crippling uncertainty to work their corrosive magic upon her fragile sanity.

Jade no longer knew or cared about the specifics of their motives. Her only driving force was survival and to come out of this in one piece.

The sudden clink of metal against metal tore through the air like a thunderclap, shattering her momentary illusion of safety. Jade's breath caught in her throat as her heart thundered in her chest.

What the hell?

It was a sound she'd heard many times, but always within the safe environment of the station or on an operation. The all-too-familiar sound of guns being checked and cocked as bodies moved close by.

No... Oh God, please no... Was this it? Had they lulled her into a false sense of security? Would she die now, with a bullet in her head?

Jade wanted to cry out, to let out a pitiful wail that might appeal to their compassionate sides... if they had any left. But she knew that any such pleas would fall upon deafened ears. These men had long since abandoned any last pretences of humanity. They meant business and got what they wanted through violence and nothing else. They were monsters who would sooner put a bullet between her eyes than show her an ounce of pity or mercy.

Jade remained silent and unmoving as footsteps hurried round her. Hot tears of dread stung at the corners of her tightly squeezed eyes, her shallow breaths coming in muted, panicked gasps. The darkness seemed to swim and pulse in time with her ragged inhalations.

She was so lost in her own panicked thoughts that it took a few seconds to notice the surrounding silence. There were no hushed tones. No guns being prepared, and no footsteps.

Jade sobbed. Had they left her? Abandoned her, never to be found?

28

What could Karen do other than wait? Shield and his assembled team were doing their best. The NCA and intelligence services were now running the show and leading the hunt for the missing officers, and yet in Karen's mind, it didn't seem enough. Everything was too slow, and with each hour that passed, her resolve and hope dwindled, but she couldn't give up, wouldn't give up.

She hoped that if it had been the other way round, and she was being held captive, that her team and the whole force would be out searching every street, abandoned house, disused farm building, and poring over every second of CCTV to find her. And that was what they were doing for Zac and Jade. Her thoughts turned to Zac. Was he holding up? Had they hurt him? Was his mental sanity in tatters? And, when they found him, would he still be the same Zac that she knew and loved? How broken would he be? There were so many questions that it twisted her stomach and made her mouth run dry.

Karen harboured the same questions about Jade. Jade was a tough and a brilliant copper, but behind that tough exterior lay a young lady still finding her place in life. Unlucky in love so many times, she'd finally found someone who liked her for being her. Open, honest, fun, and kind. *Jesus*, Karen thought, Jade didn't have it in her to survive this. It would no doubt change her on every level. The thought saddened her.

She knew the mental and emotional scars would linger long after any physical injuries disappeared. The loss of two serving officers and a key witness, as well as the countless assaults she'd experienced during her career had caused her huge turmoil in her life. Karen knew that Zac and Jade would face many months, if not years, of dark moods, doubts, nightmares, rebuilding their lives, and just doing normal day-to-day things without looking over their shoulders. On the outside they'd probably look fine. But she knew exactly what would be lurking inside.

Whatever happened, Karen knew she needed to do whatever she could to support both of them. As a victim herself, she was better placed than most therapists and mental health professionals to understand the challenges they faced.

The minutes dragged on with an excruciating slowness that seemed to impose a physical burden on Karen's shoulders. She paced the confines of the SCU in a relentless circuit, following the same route again and again until her restless steps seemed to etch grooves into the carpet fibres.

Her gaze flicked to the array of monitors and workstations like a compulsive tic, willing the screens to flare into life and give up the vital scraps of intelligence they needed. But the displays remained stubbornly unhelpful as officers pushed on with their enquiries and searches.

The soft murmurs of conversations, creaking chairs,

and clacking keyboards were like a maddening chorus that intensified Karen's feeling of helpless confinement.

Dragging her fingers through the end of her ponytail, Karen exhaled a shuddering breath and resumed her pacing for the hundredth time. She had always been impatient, never content with waiting. She thrived on action, on the heady thrill of chasing down her suspects and closing a case. This was so far removed from that, it felt alien to her.

But now, all she could do was exist in a state of maddening limbo while her mind fixated on the terrible scenarios that Zac and Jade might be enduring at the hands of their captors.

The passage of time seemed to stretch on, making the agonising hours feel like an eternity, until DCI Shield's rough voice broke through the thick tension, cutting through it like a sharpened knife. "We've got something, Karen."

Karen was at his side in an instant, her eyes focused on the sheet of paper in his hand as he pointed to it with a jab of his callused forefinger. "What have we got?"

"The NCA have come good. With the help of GCHQ and other intelligence services, they've picked up heightened mobile communications activity in a cluster just north of York, right along the southern edge of the national park." Shield elaborated, tracing the positions marked with black splotches of colour on the detailed map overlay. "Triangulation isn't accurate because of limited cell towers but it puts the signals north of this spot," he added, jabbing the map again, "a popular place for climbers and cavers."

She felt her pulse quicken as the implications slotted into place, adrenaline searing through her veins as the fog of anxiety turned into a sense of purpose. "That has to be where they're being held. It's remote, hilly with good vantage points," Karen concluded, pointing to the blob of signal hits. "It fits the topographical profile from the NCA of how Andreev's group operates back in Russia. They live and operate in the foothills away from prying eyes."

Shield grunted in agreement as he scratched his stubbly chin. "My thoughts exactly. I'll speak to..." His gruff words cut off as Karen's mobile chimed.

Frowning, she pulled the phone from her pocket and noticed an unfamiliar number on the display screen together with a text. The deceptively innocuous message that followed in the next instant threatened to rob Karen of the very ability to draw breath:

"If you want to see your friends alive, you will come alone. Instructions to follow if you accept. This is not a negotiation."

The phone slipped from her numb fingers, the heavy casing clattering against the desktop in a series of dull thuds that reverberated through her very bones. Karen was vaguely aware of Shield barking terse questions in her direction, his words seeming to emanate from a dense fog clouding her senses.

She focused completely on a single point—those few heartless lines of text that imprinted themselves in her mind in vivid, unforgettable strokes. Further confirmation that her worst fears were not subjective phantoms of anguish, but substantiated truth. The lives of Zac and Jade were hanging by a thin thread. Karen, with a sense of desperation that made her lungs burn, took in a ragged breath before summoning the strength to move her heavy, immobile legs. With so much at stake, she knew she couldn't allow herself to falter now.

Retrieving her mobile with a hand that refused to stay

steady, Karen met Shield's concerned stare. "It's them. They want me to come alone if I want Zac and Jade to live, and it's non-negotiable," she muttered, her own voice taking on a raspy edge of authority.

"Not happening," Shield protested.

With a piercing stare, Karen bore into Shield's eyes, revealing a pit of pent-up fury that seemed ready to burst at any moment.

"Listen to me! This is the only way to bring an end to this situation... fast!"

"Are you insane? You're not leading this case, nor are you remaining objective," Shield barked with a shake of his head. "You'll be playing right into their hands. There's only one way you'll come back... in a body bag along with Zac and Jade."

Karen jabbed a finger towards the wall of windows. "This is our only chance to find out where they are and get them back. These are our people, the ones we work beside every day. We owe it to them. I've sat here doing sweet FA every day. I need to be out there bringing them home."

"And risk your life and your career by going all gung-ho and cavalier on me and the rest of the team who I'd like to point out have been doing everything possible, including working overtime for free, to find them?"

"I know. Don't you think I know that, but I'm not sitting on my arse any longer waiting for a bloody miracle!" Karen shouted back, as the entire office fell silent.

Shield was about to reply when Kelly appeared at the doors with a face like thunder. "Heath, Shield, my office now!"

29

Kelly marched into her office, and Shield and Karen followed, their heads bowed as if they were naughty children who had been hauled into the headmistress's office.

Kelly slammed the door behind her and walked past them and round her desk before resting her hands on the top and leaned in. "Was that your bloody example of maintaining professional standards?" she shouted. "It was like being in a kid's playground watching two disruptive pupils fighting over who had first dibs on the climbing frame. Bloody embarrassing coming from two of my most senior detectives," she fumed. Her cheeks were bright red, and her eyes were wild with anger.

"Sorry, ma'am," Karen said. "I stepped out of line and let my emotions get the better of me. It won't happen again."

Kelly glared at Karen and then Shield. "I hope not, because I won't hesitate to put you both back down to DI if you can't get on."

Karen apologised again, but Shield remained tight-lipped, which infuriated Karen further as she drew all the flak.

"Right, would someone like to tell me what is going on?" Kelly demanded.

"Yes, ma'am. I received this message," Karen said, holding up her phone for Kelly.

"I know," Kelly said after reading the message. "Your phone is being monitored. An alert came through seconds after you received it which is why I came to find you. I'll have the high-tech unit run a trace for the origin but it's unlikely to lead to anything. The number will be from a burner phone."

"What should I reply, ma'am?"

"Nothing, Karen. This is our first contact with those who we believe are holding Zac and Jade. It will need to be discussed with the CC."

Karen nodded. "In the meantime, there's no harm in me replying with a yes? At least we'll get further instructions."

Kelly shook her head. "Absolutely not. You do not reply. This is above all of our pay grades. Two lives are in danger. For all we know it could be a trap or a hoax."

"But ma'am, I'm willing to take the risk. I could be the bait to flush them out."

Kelly slapped the desk. "Are you not listening to me, Karen? Have you really lost the plot? Every step we take from now on has to be agreed upon and signed off at the highest level."

Blowing out her cheeks, Kelly stared at the ceiling before returning her gaze to Karen. "I appreciate what you're saying. You're tough and aggressive. They were characteristics I admired and wanted in my team. But… there's a time and place for them. Now is not the time."

"I hear what you're saying, ma'am. I still don't see any

harm in replying. Their instructions could help the team and the NCA narrow down their focus of attention. It might tell me to go to a certain location and wait for further instructions." Karen paused, her breath shaky. "I know it might not be a final destination, but the fact I am there would suggest that someone would watch me. We could have surveillance teams in place."

"No, Karen! It's not happening."

Karen sensed her boss was at the end of her tether, but she had to try. She needed to push home the point or regret it for the rest of her life.

"What other options do we have, ma'am? They might be waiting for my reply, and the longer I leave it, the more suspicious they could become. The last thing I want is them cutting all communications."

Kelly stared at her two officers. "Wait outside my office while I call the CC."

Karen nodded and turned, opening the door and slipping into the corridor. Shield followed her out and closed the door behind him.

Karen glared at Shield. "You bastard. You didn't say a word in there. You hung me out to dry and let me take all the shit. You could have at least backed me up. Surely, you want this over and done with as quickly as possible?"

Shield rolled his eyes. "You let rip in there, not me. After that performance, who do you think Kelly believes to be more reliable as a senior officer? You or me?"

Anger bubbled up inside as her muscles tensed and her hands curled into fists. She wanted to run at him and gouge his eyes out. He was more snide than she ever expected. She moved away from him, folded her arms across her chest, and looked away. He had a point of course, but that didn't stop the feeling that he knew how to play the political game with senior management far better than she did. Karen's defensive tendencies divided opinions; some appreciated her tenacity, while others loathed her confrontational approach. She hoped she hadn't burnt her bridges here by going head-to-head with Kelly.

It was a long and painful twenty-five-minute wait until Kelly called them back into the office. They stood in silence waiting for Kelly to speak.

"What I'm about to say cannot be repeated outside these four walls for the time being," Kelly said, glaring at Karen, "and I don't want either of you arguing or disagreeing with me about it. This is out of my hands. I've spoken to the CC at length, and he's been in even higher-level discussions with the commissioner of the Met, the Home Secretary, and the DG at MI5. They will conduct any attempt to rescue our officers, not us. This is no longer within our control and specialist units trained in surveillance and hostage rescue will handle it."

Karen took a step back, her eyes wide, as her mouth fell open, leaving her lost for words.

Kelly noticed her reaction. "That's it. It's out of our hands. We will continue gathering evidence, and I will pass whatever we find on to the CC. That will be it for now."

Karen stood in the corridor deep in shock. Shield didn't hang around, stomping back to his team. Neither were keen to be in each other's presence as Karen slowly wandered back to her office.

30

A HEAVINESS WEIGHED upon Karen as she retreated to her office, the burden threatening to crumple her with each heavy step. The soft click of the door latch sounded so final, ushering in a suffocating silence that seemed to press in from all sides. She leaned back against the door, drawing a steadying breath as her gaze settled upon her phone.

It felt like a ticking time bomb cradled in her palm. Indecision churned within Karen's mind as conflicting thoughts waged a battle for dominance. *Was it worth it?* she questioned. Was she prepared to sacrifice her hard-earned career for the weak offer given to her? To openly defy Kelly's orders and protocols to rescue Zac and Jade? This was her weakness, and she knew it. She'd crossed the line before and couldn't help it. It appeared to be a part of her DNA make-up, an untamed rebellious streak that she had little ability to control. A part of her always baying for blood and vengeance.

Her thumb hovered over the screen, quivering as she

deliberated. It had been days since her loved ones had been ripped from their everyday lives in that single, violent instant. She couldn't let that go. With every laboured breath, Karen's fraying grasp on hope eroded a little more, her mind spiralling towards visions of the darkest, most horrific scenarios imaginable.

Were Zac and Jade still alive?

The thought alone sent a flash of anger through her. Before her resolve could crumble, Karen swiped at the phone with jerky, impulsive motions, her thumb flying across the display as she hammered out a reply.

"I need proof they're alive."

She punched the send button with a trembling fingertip. Karen's grip tightened round the phone until her knuckles turned pale with strain, the minutes slowing as she waited for... what? Confirmation of her darkest dread? Or a fragile thread of hope to cling to with the last remnants of her sanity?

The shrill chime of an incoming message caused Karen to almost fling the phone across the room in a spasm of startled reflex. Her pulse kicked into a frenzied gallop, thundering in her ears with the percussive force of kettledrums as she fumbled to open the attached file.

She gasped and her body tensed. The images that flooded the screen nearly robbed Karen of the ability to stay upright, the door a saviour. There they were—Zac and Jade, battered and bruised, their soulful eyes reflecting a trauma so harrowing that it stole the very air from her lungs in a choked exhalation.

"No ... No... No!" She slid down the door. Sobs wracked Karen's frame in heaving spasms as the reality of their suffering manifested in stark, high-definition clarity. She didn't know how long she remained slumped there, wrapped in grief and untempered fury as her fingers smeared streaks of moisture across the photos until they blurred.

Karen dragged the sleeve of her top across her blotched, tear-stained face in a rough swipe, hauling herself upright as she fought to reassert control. Clutching the phone so tightly it creaked in her white-knuckled grip, she flung open the door like a woman possessed as she ran from the room. Her team turned quizzical looks her way as she stormed past in a blur, but Karen paid them no attention as she raced off to find Kelly, determined to show her the truth. Her intention was to force her bosses into action, come whatever consequences might follow in the wake.

Without bothering to knock, she flung Kelly's office door wide, the inertia causing it to ricochet off the wall with a resonant bang as she barrelled over the threshold.

Kelly looked up annoyed at the intrusion, her expression darkening at the dishevelled sight that greeted her. "Christ, Karen, what in the bloody hell has…?"

"You have to see this," Karen blurted as she cut her off with a rasping tone, propelling her hand forward to thrust the phone into her boss's hand. "They're still alive," she said, each word laced with intensity. "But you need to see this now, ma'am."

"I know. The alert from our phone monitoring system popped up on my screen." The colour drained from Kelly's features as her gaze raked across those nightmarish images, her jaw clenching until the tendons in her neck stood out. When she at last lifted her head to meet Karen's stare, it was like staring into the heart of a raging fireball.

"You went behind my back," she hissed through gritted teeth, "After I told you not to."

Karen gave a jerky nod as more tears tumbled from her swollen and bloodshot eyes.

Kelly seemed to soften as she studied her DCI, a weary impression of grudging respect battling against the need to enforce her authority.

"You realise this is a disciplinary action? We cannot tolerate ignoring procedural instructions and direct commands from senior management on this scale," she stated in a tone of forced evenness that nonetheless carried the weight of a threat. "No matter the extenuating circumstances or emotional duress you're under."

"I know, ma'am," Karen replied. "But I'm willing to accept any punishment to see them alive and well, even if it means I lose my job. I can't stand by and see them die. Ma'am, you saw the state they're in. They won't survive much longer. I want them to know that I did everything I could to save them."

A tense silence hung between them. At long last, Kelly heaved out a sigh fraught with weariness and pinched the bridge of her nose between two fingers, the slightest tell of fraying composure. "You're too close to this entire situation; that's the fundamental issue here," Kelly muttered, almost to herself as much as to her DCI. "I should have seen something like this coming right from the bloody start. I knew you were a live wire when I considered you for our force. It's one of those rare qualities I admired in you, even if I knew it would get you into trouble."

When she looked at Karen again, her gaze emitted the cool exterior she was known for. "You need to rein in your emotions and remain clinical about this, Karen. I understand your... ill-advised overreaction stemmed from a place of despair. I get that, I really do. I'd react the same way if it was me in this situation. But this entire operation is much larger than our personal attachments."

Karen opened her mouth to speak, but Kelly raised a pre-emptive hand to silence her. "We're dealing with a group of individuals who have killed many times over, and often with firearms, not a piddly baseball bat," she pressed as she lowered her tone. "That's why conversations are happening at the absolute highest levels as we speak. We're closing in on this group with every passing minute. But we have to maintain operational integrity without compromise, Karen. We cannot allow emotion or petty impulsiveness to derail the wider investigation now… not when we're so bleeding close to getting Zac and Jade back… in one piece AND alive."

The words seemed to resonate through the confines of the office until the very air felt leaden and viscous, leaving Karen awash in a wave of shame and self-recrimination over her bout of poor judgement. Still, she lacked the energy or will to protest at her boss's stark assessment.

"You're right," she conceded in a faint, choked murmur tinged with resignation as she bobbed her head in a weary nod. "I allowed my judgement to be overridden by fear and desperation, however briefly that lapse might have lasted. It was piss-poor of me, and it won't happen again."

Kelly regarded her for a long moment, as if weighing the sincerity of the apology. Eventually, she gave a curt nod of acknowledgement.

"See that it doesn't. You do realise that I would have received an alert in the next few minutes anyway of your phone activity as it's being monitored, so thank you for coming to me straight away. We'll get them back, Karen. But it has to be done the right way."

As Karen left the office, she felt as though a momentary relief had lifted a great weight from her shoulders, only for it to be replaced by a suffocating sense of helplessness. Her impetuousness could have cost her job. All she could do now was trust Kelly's words to bring Zac and Jade home before the situation spiralled out of control.

The slimmest of lifelines remained... but it was rapidly fraying with each agonising second that trickled away.

31

After another restless night, and countless nightmares that left her staring at the dark ceiling, Karen was up, showered, and dressed before most of the SCU was in. With more time on her hands than she'd wish for, Karen headed to the canteen. She'd hardly eaten in days, and whenever she tried to keep something down, her stomach did the Irish jig, which did little to help quell the ball of anxiety that seemed to be a constant companion.

Black coffee and a few slices of toast with marmalade were all that she could face as she took a tray and found a quiet corner away from the other officers. She knew they were talking about her as they exchanged glances. There was no malice in it, perhaps more curiosity and sympathy. She assumed everyone understood her pain, maybe not completely, but a missing or injured officer always affected their colleagues. It was even worse when an officer died in the line of duty. It was only then that the actual sense of belonging to a police family hit home. A collective gathering of hearts and minds for losing one of their own.

She prayed it wouldn't come to that. In fact, she was determined it wouldn't. She took a mouthful of toast and chewed. It was as if she had lost her taste buds. Despite a generous topping of sweet marmalade, it seemed bland and tasteless. She thought about her confrontations with Kelly and raised a brow. Stupid? Yes. Out of character? Not really. When something meant so much to her, she couldn't help but cross the line.

A female officer passing by stopped by Karen's table. Probably in her mid-thirties, mousy brown hair pulled back tight in a ponytail. Never seen her before.

"Ma'am, we are all thinking of you. I promise you we are doing everything to find them. The shift will be starting soon, and I, along with the others, have been deployed to make enquiries north of the town where our suspect vehicles were last seen."

"Thank you. I appreciate it." Karen smiled as she watched the officer head over to the far side of the canteen and take a seat beside a few others. Over the course of the next twenty to thirty minutes, a few other officers stopped by with words of encouragement. Karen had to do her hardest to not cry from the outpouring of support. Even though the mood was sombre, it was heart-warming that she didn't feel so alone.

Karen spotted Anita come through the doors and smiled in her direction.

"Hey, it's good to see you up and about so early. Couldn't sleep?" Anita asked, stopping by her table and bending to give her a hug.

Karen shook her head and cupped her mug of coffee in her hands. "Not really. A few hours."

"I don't know if DCI Shield told you, but NPAS were scanning the edge of the national park for heat sources yesterday evening."

Karen placed her mug down and raised a brow. "News to me. And?"

Anita shook her head. "Nothing. It was called off after a few hours."

Karen pulled a face as her brow furrowed. "Why? Surely, they have to keep searching. It's a large area."

Anita shrugged. "Orders from above. Sorry."

Karen's phone buzzed and vibrated on the table. It was Belinda.

"Bel. Morning."

"Karen," Belinda's voice was filled with excitement as she said, "Jade has been found. She was dumped in the early hours... but she's alive."

The shock of the news left her rigid. She didn't know whether to laugh or cry. Her hand shook as she gripped her phone tighter. Her eyes widened as she stared at Anita who looked back at her through narrowed eyes.

"Where is she?"

"Been rushed to the hospital."

"Thanks." Karen cut the call and jumped up from her chair. "They've found Jade. She is safe." Her eyes moistened as the first tears of the morning spilled and trickled down her cheeks. "She's safe! They've found Jade!" Karen shouted across the canteen.

Surprise turned to a round of applause and cheers from all the officers. The relief palpable in the room.

Anita grabbed Karen's hands and squeezed tight. "Brilliant news. Any news on Zac?"

"No. But it's a start."

"I need to find the super."

"Go!"

Karen raced off as she darted in between the tables, passing a sea of smiling faces, before she disappeared through the main doors. She raced up to Kelly's office. It was still early, but Kelly would be in.

A few moments later and out of breath, Karen stood in Kelly's doorway trying to compose herself. Kelly already had a smile on her face, the news having reached her minutes ago.

"Ma'am!"

Kelly raised a hand. "Good news. I guess you've heard too."

Karen nodded. "How is she?"

"Severely dehydrated, disorientated, bruised, and sustained a few superficial injuries. The doctors are checking her over as we speak. And at the earliest opportunity, specialist officers from the intelligence services are going to do a debrief with her. We need to gather as much information as possible about the number of captors, the possible location where she might have been taken, and any other details that might help us find Zac and hold those responsible accountable for their actions."

"Ma'am, I want to see her. Please."

Kelly shook her head. "No. You could see her over a video call, but face to face is out of the question. It's too dangerous for you to leave here. You have a target on your back."

"It's not the same, ma'am. After everything she's been through. I want to be there, even if it's just for few minutes. Please." There was a desperation in Karen's voice as she begged and pleaded with her boss. "Five minutes, please? A team of AFOs could smuggle me into the hospital via the mortuary entrance. No one goes there. The entrance is discreet and hidden behind a tall brick wall. In and out in ten minutes. I'll be there and back here within an hour."

Kelly rested her hands on her hips. Her tone softened.

"You really have a problem obeying orders. I'm really not happy about any of this. If anything happens to you or the officers accompanying you, I could lose my job."

"I know. I know. It's a big ask. I wouldn't be begging you if it didn't mean that much to me. I have been worried sick about the pair of them. It would mean so much to see Jade face to face even for one minute." Karen held up her finger. "It would give me peace and hope that it won't be long until we had Zac back as well."

Kelly turned her back on Karen and walked over to the window, resting her palms on the windowsill. It seemed like an eternity to Karen as Kelly stared out of the window deep in thought. She turned, clenched her jaw and closed her eyes. "You have been under an incredible amount of strain. No one should go through what you have been experiencing in the last few days. It's a testament to your courage, determination, and sheer bloody-mindedness that you held it together... just about. Yes, you've been a huge thorn in my side, but I expected nothing less from you."

Karen took that as a compliment of sorts and smiled as embarrassment flushed her cheeks.

"Against my better judgement, we'll do this. I'll arrange for one team of AFOs to go with you in the back of an unmarked Transit van. There will also be an advanced escort of AFOs, and a second team following behind you. Everyone will be in plain clothes, unmarked cars, and a silent approach. Jade is already under armed guard, so I'll make sure they have secured the entrance by the mortuary before you arrive."

Karen let out a deep breath. A surge of adrenaline and excitement coursed through her veins that made her skin tingle. She felt positively euphoric. "Thank you, ma'am. Thank you."

Kelly jabbed a finger in Karen's direction. "Don't thank me until you get back in one piece. I'll make the calls now. Be ready in ten minutes."

She nodded and ran out of Kelly's room before uttering another word.

32

THE BACK of the Transit was hot and stuffy. Karen had to grip on to the seat as the vehicle swerved from side to side. They had left the station compound via a rear exit once officers patrolling the grounds had scanned the area.

Karen couldn't contain herself as they covered the short distance. There were four AFOs in the van's rear with her. None of them spoke a word, all lost in their own thoughts as they mentally prepped themselves. Even words of gratitude from the deepest part of her heart didn't seem sufficient, considering how much they were risking their lives for her.

Minutes later the van lurched as it took a sharp right and turned in to the mortuary compound. The van spun round and reversed up to the double doors. The officers readied themselves, their movements sharp and controlled. Two officers exited the rear of the van first and checked their surroundings before giving Karen the nod. She jumped out of the back, the other two AFOs following behind her. The doors of the corridor leading to the mortuary entrance swung open, and a further two AFOs met the party.

Together they hurried along the corridor, their footsteps in unison tapping on the tiled floor which created a crescendo of noise that at times overwhelmed Karen. Other than her trip to Wakefield prison, she'd spent the last few days being cooped up and hardly stretched her legs, let alone seen anything beyond the walls of the block she was in. And now she was being frogmarched at speed surrounded by six heavily armed and highly trained firearms officers. They stopped at the service lifts and waited a few seconds before the doors opened. It was big enough to accommodate all of them as they took the lift up to the next floor.

Once out, the group made their way along a private corridor only accessible to hospital staff. The pace was quick and intense, Karen breathing hard, perhaps not so much through exertion, but anticipation.

They finally stopped by a door to a room which had no windows. Two further plain-clothed AFOs stood guard either side of the entrance. Karen felt like an army surrounded her. They all paused and the lead AFO opened the door and let Karen through, closing the door behind her.

Seeing Jade took her breath away. Gone was the bright, attractive, and cheerful woman who had become her best friend. She looked ten years older, her vibrant spirit dimmed by the depravities she had endured. The ordeal had left her with bedraggled hair, a face marred with bruises, and sunken cheekbones.

Jade turned her head on the pillow to see Karen. They both burst into tears as Karen rushed to be beside her, wrapping her hand inside hers and squeezing it tight. Snot trails and tears mixed in an unsightly mess which gathered on Karen's top lip. She wiped it away with the back of her hand as her sobs filled the room.

"My God. I've been so worried and sick. I can't tell you how good it is to see you," Karen said. Her words sounded pathetic, but she didn't know what else to say.

Jade's tears fell from her eyes and rolled down to her ears before dropping on to the pillow. Her body shook as the shock surfaced. She tried to talk, but the words wouldn't come.

"Sssh. Save your breath. It's a relief that you're safe. I haven't got long. Outside, I have an army of AFOs who smuggled me in. The boss didn't want me to come, but I insisted, so I only have a few minutes."

"I... I... thought I was going to die," Jade muttered, her voice broken and weak. "As soon as I heard the guns being prepared, I thought they were going to kill me. Then everything fell silent for a while, but they came back and picked me up, stuffed me in the boot of a car before driving somewhere and dumping me."

Karen noticed how Jade stared at the ceiling, and it was clear from her darting eye movements that she was doing her best to recall her last moments with them.

"Listen, don't worry about anything. Specialist officers will visit to do a full debrief with you. Did you see Zac?"

"What?" Jade replied. Worry lines creased her forehead.

Karen sighed. "They took Zac too."

Jade turned and stared at Karen as her eyes misted over. She shook her head. "No. I didn't hear him or see him. I don't know where he is. I'm so sorry, Karen."

Karen rubbed Jade's arm and tried to brush away Jade's concerns, but inside, the news crushed her further. "Hey, you have nothing to be sorry for. I bet Zac is really giving them a hard time. You know what he's like. I feel sorry for the men who are holding him." Karen let out a weak laugh. "We'll get him back soon."

A few minutes later, there was a knock on the door. Karen knew her time was up.

"I've got to go. You get some rest, and I'll video-call you later?"

Jade nodded and closed her eyes.

Karen kissed Jade on the forehead before heading to the door. She rested her fingers on the handle and looked over her shoulder. Jade's injuries on the outside were nothing compared to the injuries inside. She wondered if she'd ever get her friend back, the Jade she loved so much. As Karen opened the door, a sea of impatient faces greeted her, with the AFOs ready to take her back. As they left in convoy along the corridor, she noticed two men dressed in jeans and hoodies coming their way, each holding a briefcase. An AFO was escorting them. Jade's debrief was about to start.

33

Karen returned to her office, emotions swirling within her. Relief at finally seeing Jade alive mixed with guilt over the happiness she was experiencing while knowing Zac was still in the clutches of his captors. She sank into her chair, feeling drained yet strangely energised. Was this really the start of the end?

She sat in silence for the next hour processing the visit. So much had happened in the space of a few hours. Karen couldn't shake the haunting image of Jade—a mere shadow of her former self. Pushing herself to her feet, Karen made her way to the SCU where the team had assembled. A hush fell over them as she entered, their expectant gazes piercing her with an unspoken need for answers.

"I've seen her," Karen began, her voice thick with an amalgam of emotions. "Jade's alive and that's the main thing, but..." she trailed off, struggling to find the words to convey the disturbing reality. Clearing her throat, she pressed on. "She's in terrible shape—beaten, malnourished, and traumatised. It's like she aged ten years in a few days."

A collective sigh rippled through the room, a mix of relief and concern etching itself on the team's faces. Bel spoke up, her brow furrowed. "But Zac... Is there any word? Did she see him? Talk to him?"

Karen shook her head, feeling the guilt resurface. "Nothing I'm afraid. I only had a few minutes with her. Jade didn't know he'd been taken or his whereabouts."

An uneasy silence descended, punctuated only by the occasional shuffling of feet or clearing of throats as many officers returned to their desks. Excusing herself, Karen went in search of Kelly, needing to debrief her boss on the visit and to thank her again. But the superintendent's office was empty, and the door ajar. Karen frowned. The ACC must have tied up Kelly in meetings again.

Returning to her own office, Karen called Anita. She was desperate to share the good news.

"Karen... any news?"

"I've seen her, Anita. Jade."

The release of a deep breath filtered through the line. "Oh, thank God... How did you get out? You're under lock and key here?"

"Not easy, but I pleaded with the super," Karen said. "She gave in but sent me with an entire armed convoy to see Jade at the hospital for a few minutes. I guess it was better than nothing and put my mind at peace a bit."

"I don't care about the details," Anita replied, the relief palpable in her tone. "Knowing she's still with us..."

Karen paused and nodded before continuing. "She's been through hell, Anita. Beaten, starved... she looks ten years older. But she's a fighter."

The call continued for almost thirty minutes, as Anita did her best to lift Karen's spirit before Karen excused herself, promising to pass along any other updates. As she ended the call, her desk phone rang—Karen was needed in the main briefing room immediately. Frowning, Karen made her way down the corridor. What recent development awaited her now? What had happened in the short time she'd been away?

She pushed through the door to find an unexpectedly sombre gathering—Kelly, DCI Shield, Wendy from the NCA, and even the assistant chief constable. A knot of trepidation formed in the pit of Karen's stomach as she took a seat, the heavy silence only added to the charged atmosphere.

"Thanks for coming, Karen. We're all needed for this briefing," the ACC said, breaking the awkward silence that hung between everyone round the table.

A sharp rap at the door broke the stillness as a uniformed officer entered, flanked by two men dressed in casual attire yet carrying themselves with an unmistakable air of crisp professionalism.

"Allow me to introduce..." the ACC began.

But the introduction was unnecessary. Karen's eyes widened as realisation set in—these were the same two individuals she had noticed at the hospital as she left.

"Captain Henry Bird, and Sergeant Craig Roberts, gentlemen from the SAS, British military," the ACC continued, confirming Karen's suspicion. "They have a... vested interest in this situation and are here after the Home Secretary contacted the CC. High level discussions took place and the Home Secretary approved the involvement of the SAS in the rescue of our officers."

One man nodded curtly before they both took a seat. Pleasantries aside, Captain Bird began. "Based on the insights provided by your colleague together with information given to us by senior intelligence officials, we'll be spearheading the reconnaissance and rescue operation."

Karen's breath caught in her throat as the words registered. The SAS—the UK's most elite special forces unit—was taking over the operation to recover Zac.

"What intelligence?" Karen blurted out.

The ACC responded to her question with disapproving looks.

Bird shook his head. "For operational reasons, it's not something we can discuss. The fewer people that know, the better."

"We're not the enemy here," Karen replied.

"With all due respect, you have several hundred officers deployed. We do not have the time nor resources to vet every single officer. It's not unheard of for a rogue officer to provide intelligence to the same people we are tasked to track down."

Karen didn't know what to make of that statement. "There are no leaks here," she snapped.

Bird raised a brow.

The assistant chief constable interrupted, his voice brooking no argument. "They have the experience and resources required to navigate this situation. I needn't remind anyone here of the stakes involved."

Karen stiffened and leaned forward in her seat wanting to say something but doubted it would go down too well as she was already in the doghouse with her boss, but Captain Bird raised a hand to pre-empt her objection. "I can appreciate your concern, DCI. But our squadrons have conducted countless hostile R & R operations round the globe, even when outnumbered one hundred to one by enemy combatants in many regions."

His lip curled in a mirthless smile. "Situations not dissimilar to this one. Except our missions in Afghan valleys like Panji and Sangin resulted in zero British casualties."

Karen felt her throat tighten as the implications sank in. "And the hostages? How many survived your... operations?"

The ACC sighed in frustration, and Kelly raised a brow in Karen's direction, her displeasure clear.

The two men exchanged a guarded look before Bird responded. "Casualties are... an unfortunate reality. But our success rate is among the highest of any elite force in the world. We're talking of a mission to rescue one hostage, not ten. So the odds are in our favour."

She opened her mouth to protest further, but the ACC cut her off with a curt motion. "You'll send the message agreeing to the meet on their terms. That's an order, DCI."

With jaw clenched, Karen could only nod tightly in agreement as she withdrew her phone with trembling hands. There would be no reasoning with these hardened military professionals—they followed a different code, one forged in global conflict zones. As her thumbs tapped out the fateful response setting the wheels in motion, Karen could only hope that their single-minded determination to succeed wouldn't inadvertently lead to further tragedy before this nightmare ended. Her boyfriend's life was on the line. It might not mean much to them, or to those round the table with her, but it meant the world to her. She didn't want a bloodbath. Just Zac's safe return.

Now they could only brace for the consequences, whatever they might be.

34

AFTER THE BRIEFING, Karen left the room and returned to her office. Though the others were still there along with the members of the SAS, the atmosphere felt stifling. No one spoke as they all sat in silence waiting. Though Kelly's preference was for her DCI to remain in the room, Karen had said she needed the space to be on her own. She'd also promised to return to the briefing room as soon as Zac's captors replied.

With her door shut, and the drone of voices somewhere further down the corridor muffled, it gave Karen the opportunity to process and come to terms with everything that had happened in the last few hours. The news about Jade, seeing her face to face, the tidal wave of emotions she'd experienced, and then to top it off, sitting across the table with two members of the Special Air Service. It was the stuff that movies were made of, and it reminded her of a movie she had watched many years ago, which featured Lewis Collins as an SAS officer in *Who Dares Wins*. Though she loved the movie and had watched it many times, she remembered the carnage as the SAS tore through the building, guns blazing. Karen prayed it wouldn't be like that when they rescued Zac.

She tapped her fingers on the desk. Each minute felt like an hour. She glanced at her phone dozens of times. Had the message gone through? Were the captors in such a remote location that reception was poor at the best of times? Or, and more likely, were they playing a waiting game to show that they were in control and calling the shots?

"Come on, come on. Hurry up." Karen rose from her chair. Her legs were restless. She needed the loo. With her phone in her back pocket, she strode down the hallway and disappeared into the ladies. A minute later she was out of the cubicle and standing in front of the sink. Her reflection in the mirror took her by surprise. Dark brown circles framed her eyes. Her face had lost colour, and her eyes appeared lifeless. She looked like a walking mannequin. And it was all down to stress, anxiety, and a lack of sleep. Everyone kept telling her to rest, but how could she? Jade was back, and that was good. How could she sleep when Zac was going through such an ordeal?

Turning on the tap, she splashed cold water over her face, welcoming the jolt to her system. The cold water was like a slap in the face, waking her from her drowsy state. She grabbed a few paper towels and dabbed at the moisture, enjoying the coolness of her skin. Her phone buzzed in her back pocket and almost scared her. She tossed the towels to one side and hurried to pull out her phone.

They had replied.

Karen read through the text.

"Will send coordinates shortly. You must come alone with no police backup, no phone, no radio, or tracking devices. We will be watching you. Any sign of others and your boyfriend will

die. It is not a threat. It is a promise. We will post him back to you in pieces. Then you'll be next."

She read the message twice, each time lingering on every word. Her mouth went dry, and her palms became clammy. This is it. This is the start of the end. She turned and headed for the door when another message pinged through. It was an attachment and as she opened it, she gasped. It was another picture of Zac. But this time his face looked a mess. They had beaten him again. Karen closed her eyes, desperate to hold back the wave of tears and sadness that threatened to consume her. She needed to stay strong and objective.

Seeing a picture of Zac only angered her further. She wanted to be there holding the gun when the SAS found Zac. Every cell of her being wanted his captors dead. She couldn't imagine life without Zac now. Her mind turned to Summer. She wanted to call. But what would she say? As she left the ladies and headed back to the briefing room, she dialled Summer's number.

Summer answered on the first ring. "Karen, have they found Dad?"

The question hit her like a thunderbolt in the middle of her chest and stole her breath. There was so much expectancy and anticipation in Summer's voice that she now regretted making the call.

"Not yet, darling. Real soon. We've found Jade. Now we have a better idea of where your dad is." Karen bit her lip when she heard Summer squeal and cry.

"I want my dad back. Please, Karen. Get him back. I miss him."

Karen listened but couldn't understand Summer's words as sniffs and further wails drowned them out.

She was about to say something when Michelle came on the line.

"Was there a specific reason behind your call or did you decide to call for the sake of it and further upset Summer?" Michelle snapped. "*My* daughter has been staring at her phone for days waiting for news of her dad, and you call with... nothing. What was the bloody point?"

Karen understood the frustration and anger in Michelle's tone. She didn't blame her. Perhaps it had been a foolish thing to call, and, she had made a few poor decisions on the back of her emotions. She could add this to the list.

"Sorry, Michelle, I didn't call to upset her. I've been thinking about her all the time, and it must be awful for her. We are getting close to finding Zac. I just wanted to let her know she was in my thoughts. And I wish I could see her."

"I'll pass that on for you," Michelle replied, before cutting off the call.

Karen's jaw dropped as she stared at the blank screen. Even in such a difficult time, Michelle still couldn't be civil to Karen. While she had been on a call, another text had come through with the coordinates.

She hurried back to the briefing room.

35

"I HAVE THE LOCATION," Karen shouted as she burst through the door of the briefing room. Her entrance was anything but professional as she took a few deep breaths to steady her racing heart. Those round the table shifted in their seats, a ripple of excitement and energy buzzing through the room.

The ACC turned to Captain Bird. "It's over to you now. This is your operation."

Karen handed her phone to Captain Bird, who scanned the message before passing the device to his sergeant.

Sergeant Roberts tapped away on his laptop before he swivelled the screen round for his superior to view. They studied the topography for a moment, each of them pointing out certain elements that were worth considering before Bird took over.

"Based on our observations, the location appears to be secluded with no residences within a mile in any direction, indicating that the captors are aware of the safety of this starting point, although it is unlikely to be the final destination."

"Why not?" Karen asked. Though a part of her wanted to stay silent, she needed answers for everything.

"It is standard practice for captors in this situation. They will move you round to see if you are being followed. Of course you will be, but they won't know that or see anything suspicious. Those who are meeting you will be heavily armed. From what we know of this group of individuals, they are ruthless, determined, and will fight until the last breath."

The news did little to dampen the ball of nerves spinning out of control in Karen's chest. She felt jittery.

"You have a pair of jeans with you, don't you?" Bird asked Karen.

She pursed her lips. The question seemed odd, but she nodded.

"We'll be replacing the metal button on your jeans with a small tracking device disguised as a button. Don't worry, they won't be able to pick it up with any handheld scanners. The tracking device is designed to remain undetected. This will allow us to track you from a distance without being seen."

It wasn't the answer she expected, nor did she like the prospect of being isolated with no backup close by. She wasn't accustomed to it but had to trust the captain's words.

Bird stood up and stretched his legs. He was a tall man, nearly six feet tall, with broad shoulders, stubbly beard, and a commanding presence. Someone who you would listen to when his blue eyes glared at you. "We will have two six-man teams following on the eastern and western flanks of Karen's position in unmarked vehicles disguised as DPD courier vans. They will be our surveillance and rescue teams. We will also use a sniper team. If there is any risk to you, they will eliminate the threat from more than half a mile away. The first the targets would know about our presence is when one of them hits the floor minus his brains. In the shock and confusion that would follow, we'd take out the rest."

"We are not looking for a bloodbath here," the ACC interrupted.

Bird nodded. "Neither are we. This is purely a precautionary measure and only to be used as a last resort," he stressed.

The more Karen heard, the more it terrified her. The entire operation was out of her hands, and she was a tactical pawn. Did they view her as collateral damage if shit hit the fan?

"In terms of rescuing your officer," Bird said, addressing the ACC, "other than the surveillance and rescue teams on the ground, we will deploy a backup six-man troop by helicopter once we discover the actual location. Our intention is shock and awe, to create as much confusion as possible, which in our experience leads to disorientation and ineffectiveness by the captors. It makes it easy for our units to remove them with the least amount of fuss."

The ACC chewed his lip and nodded, seemingly happy with their approach as he glanced at the others round the table. Wendy from the NCA remained silent throughout the whole discussion as did Shield who looked a bit bewildered. His eyes didn't leave the two SAS officers throughout the whole discussion. Was that because he was in awe of them? Or did he hate the fact that someone was taking away the final acts in this investigation from him, and he wouldn't be able to bask in the glory?

Captain Bird continued to discuss the finer points of the operation before he took a seat. He once again addressed the ACC. "We'd like teams of your AFOs to be stationed one mile away on all roads leading to the final location. The intention is to form an outer ring to stop any captors escaping."

The ACC sat back in his chair and puffed out his chest. "Consider it done. I have already drafted in over fifty AFOs from across the North to help. I can also confirm that two NPAS units will be five minutes away to track things from the air. They can move at a moment's notice."

"Thank you. That would be helpful. I must remind all of you we are dealing with difficult terrain. It's rugged and provides little in the way of cover. My teams are going to find this operation challenging and it will be hard for them to stay covert and unseen, but they've done it before and they'll do it again. You could be out in the middle of the field with a covert surveillance unit just yards from you and you wouldn't even know they were there. They can remain hidden for days."

"Impressive," the ACC commented.

Sergeant Roberts packed away his laptop and files as Captain Bird stood.

"Any questions?" Bird asked. His request was met with a wall of silence.

Karen had been involved in surveillance operations during her time in the Met, but this was on a whole new level and the planning left her bewildered, and truth be told, a little intimidated.

"Karen, have you got any questions?" Captain Bird asked.

Karen wanted to express her petrifying fear, a fear unlike any she had experienced before, and her terror that it might all culminate in a hail of bullets and a bloodbath. However, she couldn't display any sign of weakness at such a crucial stage. From somewhere deep within her, she needed to draw on her strength, resilience, and determination to see this through. She needed Zac back. "No, nothing from me."

Bird nodded. "Right, let's get you ready."

36

Once Karen changed, the "tracking device" button was fitted on her jeans, and Captain Bird finished a flurry of calls ensuring that everything was in place, he prepared for Karen to leave. Karen took a quick detour promising to be back in a few minutes. She raced to the SCU where many of her team were busy with their own lines of enquiry. Although she wanted to go in and break the news of the operation, Kelly and the ACC had sworn her to secrecy. Not wishing to piss them off any further, Karen lurked in the corridor and stared through the glass partition.

She felt melancholy. Karen didn't know what the next few hours had in store for her, and whether she would see her team again. A heady mixture of dread, fear, and anticipation left her light-headed. Her stomach churned and her bowels twitched. This was so far left field, her mind struggled to process the predicament she found herself in. Going head-to-head with an armed criminal gang was bad enough, but to be thrust into the middle of a military operation was something else. It was as if the hopes of the force and every police officer up and down the country rested on her shoulders.

She already missed them as she spotted Bel discussing something with Ed, with Ty, Clare, and Ned on the phones. Right now, she could do with being surrounded by some friendly faces. Hopefully later. She cast her eye on the team one last time before she turned and headed back down the corridor. She disappeared down the stairwell before stepping out into the chilly late afternoon. Her moist breath hung in the air as the two SAS officers, Kelly, DCI Shield, Wendy, and the ACC, all gathered round her. She didn't want to admit it, but it felt like a last farewell which only added to the gloom.

They wished her good luck, including Shield, which Karen thought must have been hard for him to say. Karen got in her car, studied the instructions printed out for her, and set off. She glanced in her rear-view mirror and watched the figures disappear from view.

It wasn't long before she left the outskirts of the city, and the busy roads were soon replaced by narrow country roads lined with hedgerow on either side. With the light fading, it felt like they were closing in on her as she drove. She prayed that Captain Bird's unit was able to track her movements well enough in the dark. It might have helped his officers with remaining covert and harder to spot, but it played right into the hands of Zac's captors who could melt away into the darkness much easier.

Karen navigated the winding roads, her eyes fixed on the black line of tarmac caught in her headlights as she neared the designated meeting point. The darkness seemed to press in from all sides, broken only by the weak illumination of her headlights. She tried to calm her racing thoughts, but the eerie stillness of the night did little to ease her growing sense of unease.

This is bloody madness, she thought.

A quick glance at the instruction sheet on her passenger seat confirmed she'd arrived. Karen slowed the car and turned into a small lay-by. The crunch of gravel beneath her tyres sounded unnaturally loud in the otherwise silent landscape. She put the car in park and turned off the engine, plunging herself into an oppressive, pitch-black quietness.

Glancing at the dashboard clock, Karen saw she was a few minutes early. She took a deep breath to steady her nerves. The weight of the situation hung heavily upon her, the knowledge that Zac's life depended on the outcome of this meeting.

"What am I doing? Shit." Karen shivered as fear paralysed her. "You can do this. Pull yourself together."

Karen peered out into the darkness, her eyes straining to make out any signs of movement. A small glimmer of light from the moon as it appeared through a break in the clouds allowed her to spot the faint outline of trees in the distance, their branches swaying gently in the cool night breeze. Despite the stillness, she couldn't shake off the sensation of being under surveillance, as if unseen eyes were closely watching her every move. She only hoped it was the SAS.

Unease prickled at the back of her neck as Karen scanned the road in both directions. There were no headlights, no indications of another human presence in this isolated stretch of countryside. The only vehicle she had encountered in the last few minutes was a solitary DPD delivery van that had passed her prior to reaching the lay-by. At the time, Karen had barely registered the van's presence, her mind too focused on the impending meeting. But now, in the suffocating solitude of the lay-by, the memory of that encounter reminded her she wasn't alone.

Karen shook her head, trying to dislodge the paranoid thoughts that threatened to take hold. She knew her mind was playing tricks on her, the stress and anxiety of the situation amplifying every insignificant detail. The whistle of wind and the odd screech from God knows what left her nervy. She needed to keep her composure and stay focused on the task at hand.

Her thoughts turned to Zac, to the unimaginable horrors he must be enduring at the hands of his captors. The idea itself of him suffering, alone, and afraid, caused Karen's heart to tighten in her chest. She had to stay strong for him, to see this through no matter the cost. Failure wasn't an option. Karen knew that if she allowed her fears to consume her, if she let doubt and indecision paralyse her, then she would seal Zac's fate. She had to be the one to save him, to bring him back.

Suddenly, her head jerked up, her eyes wide as she saw a pair of headlights approaching in the distance. Not one set, but two. Was this them? It had to be. They grew steadily larger, closing in on her location. Karen's heart thumped hard as adrenaline surged through her veins like an electric current. This was it, the moment of truth. All the planning and all the risks she'd taken had led to this pivotal encounter.

She stepped out of the car on shaky legs, the chill of the night air biting through her clothing. Karen wrapped her arms round her chest for warmth and protection.

As the approaching vehicles drew closer, Karen took a deep breath, steeling herself for what was to come. She silently offered a prayer, pleading with whatever higher power might be listening to watch over her, to guide her steps in the right direction. For Zac, Karen would go through any obstacle to confront the depths of human depravity. Until she had secured his safety and brought the bastards who had taken him to justice, she would not rest. Even if it meant sacrificing her own safety, her own future, Karen would gladly pay that price.

The headlights grew blinding as the vehicles came to a stop just a few metres away. Karen raised a hand to shield her eyes, while her heart pounded so loudly that she was sure it could be heard over the idling engines. This was the beginning of the end, the first step in a journey that would either lead to Zac's rescue or their deaths. But Karen was ready, her resolve unwavering in the face of the unknown.

37

Karen stood close to her car, readying herself.

Why are they not getting out? Too suspicious? Have we blown the operation already?

She imagined the cars roaring off again, spooked by something.

Please God, no.

The doors swung open, and several men emerged, their faces obscured by balaclavas. They moved with a cautious urgency, their body language betraying their wariness of the situation.

Karen's breath caught in her throat as she noticed the outline of handguns pointed in her direction. The men fanned out, taking up lookout positions, while two others approached her. Their eyes darted round, scanning the darkness for any signs of a trap. Without a word, the two men searched Karen, their hands patting her down. She flinched at their touch, her skin crawling with revulsion as a hand squeezed her crotch. One produced a handheld scanner and brushed it against her from the top of her head to the tips of her toes. Once satisfied that she was unarmed, he produced a hood and placed it over her head, plunging her in to complete darkness.

Disoriented and frightened, Karen felt someone prod and encourage her from behind, pulling her along by her arm, and forcing her at gunpoint to abandon her car and climb into another vehicle. The door slammed shut, and the car took off, the sudden movement causing her to lurch in her seat. The men never spoke a word. The entire journey took place in silence. As the car snaked through the narrow lanes, braking sharply on tight bends before accelerating away, it gave her little to go on as she was tossed from side to side.

After what felt like an eternity, the car came to a stop. Karen tried to tune in to her surroundings. But there was nothing. An empty silence. No cars, no machinery, not even the bleating of sheep. They hauled her out and transferred her to a second vehicle before continuing the journey. Karen prayed her saviours weren't far behind. It was another journey in silence before it came to a stop. Time seemed irrelevant. She did not know how long she'd been with Zac's captors now. Twenty minutes? Half an hour? She was thrust forward when the car came to an abrupt halt. And she soon found herself in a third car, her sense of direction completely lost.

This journey didn't last long before they pulled her from her seat. Scared and unsteady on her feet, the men led her on foot. The ground beneath her was uneven and grassy, causing her to stumble and trip. Exposed tree roots her nemesis. Each time she fell, firm hands gripped her arms and hoisted her back to her feet with an aggressive yank. But she sensed they were on an incline as each step became harder. A trek through the hills?

As they walked, the ground beneath her feet changed, the soft, grassy earth giving way to a harder, more uneven surface. The air grew colder, and the sounds of their footsteps echoed round her, suggesting they had entered a cave. It definitely wasn't an underground chamber because the journey had been uphill all the way. The men remained silent, their presence announced only by the occasional rustle of clothing or the crunch of gravel under their boots. Karen's ragged breath did little to drown out her thoughts, her imagination running wild with the horrors that might await her. Then she realised with scary intensity. What if the tracking device disguised as a button didn't work inside the cave? Would they still find her? Was she alone?

After what seemed like an eternity, they came to a halt. Karen gasped as someone forcefully pushed her into a chair. She strained her ears, trying to make sense of her surroundings, but the only sound was the intensity of her breath that left her face damp and clammy.

Sitting there, shrouded in darkness and surrounded by her captors, Karen tried to steel herself for whatever lay ahead. She thought of Zac, of the strength he must be clinging to in the face of unimaginable adversity. She gasped as a thought crossed her mind. Was he there too?

In the oppressive silence of the cave, Karen waited, her every nerve stretched taut with anticipation. She knew that the next few moments would be critical, that the fate of both her and Zac hung in the balance. Where were the SAS? They'd promised to track her every step and be close by. How could they be close by in a bloody cave? Had they lost her location? Was that why they weren't here? The thought alone terrified her. If that was the case, then what? She had no plan B. No escape plan. And no means of fighting against such heavily armed thugs.

Shit.

Karen's heart hammered against her ribs, each beat a

loud echo in the cavernous silence. She clenched her fists, feeling the cold sweat on her palms. *Zac, where are you? Are you feeling this same paralysing fear?* A shiver raced down her spine as the darkness seemed to press closer, whispering of impending dangers yet unseen. But she had to stay strong. For Zac. For herself. Fear would not win, no matter how powerful it became.

Her breath caught as she braced for what was to come, the weight of shared fate pressing down like the darkness itself.

38

A MAN YANKED off Karen's hood. She blinked, her eyes struggling to adjust to the dim, flickering light of the cave. There were small lamps dotted round, casting eerie shadows on the damp, cold walls. More than a dozen men, maybe more, filled the cave, their faces obscured by balaclavas, armed with an array of handguns and AK47s. The sight sent a wave of icy terror through Karen's veins. She'd seen nothing like it in her life.

"Where am I?" Karen demanded, her voice echoing off the rocky walls. "And where the hell is Zac? I've done everything you asked. Now it's your turn to hold up your end of the bargain."

A deafening silence greeted her questions. The men remained still, their weapons trained on her, their fingers hovering over the triggers. Not an ounce of emotion between them.

"I said, where's Zac?" Karen repeated, her voice rising with anger and frustration. "You aren't all bloody deaf and dumb."

Still nothing.

The men parted, and the sound of footsteps echoed from the darkness. A figure emerged from the shadows, and as the dim light illuminated their face, Karen's heart lurched.

"Well, well, well. Look who it is. DCI Karen Heath," Sally Connell said, a malicious grin spread across her face.

Icy-cold shock struck Karen speechless, her mind reeling with a maelstrom of anger, betrayal, and disbelief. She glared at Sally with hatred burning in her eyes. "Where. Is. Zac?" Karen asked again. Each word dripped with barely contained rage.

Connell snapped her fingers, and the men behind her dragged in a hooded figure, forcing them into a chair opposite Karen. With a swift, violent motion, they removed the hood, revealing Zac's battered and bruised face. He looked at Karen through bloodshot, pain-filled eyes, his expression a mix of desperation and exhaustion, his strength drained.

Karen's heart lurched, and her blood boiled with an all-consuming fury. She wanted nothing more than to wrap her hands round Connell's throat and squeeze the life out of her, to make the evil woman pay for every ounce of pain she had inflicted. But even that didn't feel like enough. She wanted Sally Connell to endure a slow and excruciating death.

Connell revelled in Karen's reaction; her smugness was palpable, and she tossed her head back and laughed. "Consider this payback for what happened to my brother," she said, her voice laced with venom. "My new alliance with the Russians has made me the most powerful woman in the criminal underworld. And now, I'm going to make you suffer like never before."

One man stepped forward and threw a noose over

Zac's head and pulled it tight, causing him to gasp and struggle for air. Karen screamed, her heart pounding so hard she thought it might burst from her chest. She launched from her chair, but men on either side of her quickly restrained her and pushed her back into her seat. "Stop!" Karen screamed. "He's not done anything to you. If you want to hurt someone, then hurt me, but let Zac go!"

"Speaking of suffering," Connell said as she walked round Karen, her words cutting through Karen's panic like a razor. "How's your dear friend Steve Nugent doing these days?"

Karen's mind raced, confusion and dread filling her thoughts as her brow furrowed.

"I was devastated to hear about his tragic motorbike accident with that van or car, or whatever it was," Connell continued, her voice dripping with false sympathy. "I instructed Grozev's men not to hurt him excessively, but I suppose our definitions of 'not too much' differ quite a bit."

The revelation hit Karen like a sledgehammer as she gasped, her anger reaching a boiling point. She had never once considered the possibility that Sally Connell was behind Steve's accident.

"Hurting Steve, abducting Jade and Zac… it was all a carefully crafted message," Connell explained, her eyes gleaming with sadistic pleasure. "A reminder that I can hurt you whenever I please without laying a finger on you. That I have the power to make your life a living hell, and there's nothing you or anyone else can do."

Karen's rage consumed her, and she lunged forward again, desperate to get her hands on Sally Connell. But the men were too quick, grabbing her and slamming her back into the chair with brutal force that knocked the air out of her.

"Ah, ah, ah," Connell tutted, wagging her finger at Karen like a disapproving schoolteacher. "Let's not do anything silly now, Karen. Wouldn't want anything terrible to happen to poor Zac, would we?" She laughed. "I think you're carrying enough guilt already. Being responsible for Zac's death would send you to the loony bin for life. And then Summer would lose all her favourite people..."

"Don't you dare lay a finger on Summer. I'll fucking kill you with my bare hands, you evil bitch."

Connell nodded to one man, who tightened the noose round Zac's neck, causing him to choke and sputter. Karen's heart raced with terror, tears of frustration and fear stinging her eyes.

"You're a sick monster," Karen spat, her voice shaking with anger. "I swear to God, I'll..."

"You'll what exactly?" Connell interrupted, her tone dripping with condescension. "You'll arrest me? Throw me in prison? Oh, Karen. You don't know who you're dealing with. I own this city now. And most importantly, I own you."

She leaned in close, her face only inches away from Karen's. "You're nothing more than a pawn in my game. A tiny, insignificant piece on my chessboard. And I can remove you from the board whenever I want. All it takes is this. One. Simple. Call." Connell straightened up, a cruel smile playing on her lips. "But don't worry, Karen. I'm not going to kill you. Not yet, anyway. Where's the fun in that? No, I'm going to make you watch as I destroy everything and everyone you love. Starting with Zac. That's why I needed you here. I wanted to see the fear in your eyes. The desperation in your voice. And the sheer hopelessness of your situation."

She nodded to the man holding the noose, who tightened it further. Zac's face turned a sickening shade of purple as he gasped for air, his body convulsing. Spittle flying from his mouth.

"No!" Karen screamed, tears streaming down her face. "Stop! Please! I'll do anything you want. Just stop."

Connell held up a hand, and the man loosened the noose, allowing Zac to take a shuddering breath. "You see, Karen? This is what actual power looks like. The power to give life and take it away. The power to make you beg and plead and grovel at my feet."

Karen's mind raced as she searched for a way out of this nightmare. But before she could stall or come up with a plan, a deafening explosion rocked the cave. The force of the blast sent Connell flying backward. Karen and Zac's chairs toppled over, sending them crashing to the ground as clouds of dust and smoke filled the space.

Chaos erupted as men rushed towards the cave entrance, their shouts mingling with the sound of gunfire and the blinding flashes of flash-bang grenades. Karen struggled to her feet, disoriented with a ringing in her ears and a pounding in her chest, as she watched Connell pull a handgun from the pocket of her coat and charge towards her with murder in her eyes.

The cave became a war zone, filled with smoke, dust, and the deafening echoes of violence as a battle raged. Karen knew that the next few moments would be the most critical of her life, that the fate of both her and Zac hung in the balance. She braced herself for the fight of her life, determined to do whatever it took to survive, to save Zac, and to make Connell pay for her crimes. As the chaos raged round them, Karen felt a sense of grim determination settle over her. This was her moment, her chance to take back control, and she would not let it slip through her fingers.

With a last burst of strength, Karen lunged forward, tackling Sally to the ground as she raised her gun to fire. The two women grappled on the rocky floor of the cave, trading blows and scratches as they fought for control of the weapon. Karen's training kicked in, and she disarmed Connell with a swift, precise strike to the wrist. The gun clattered to the ground.

Karen scrambled to retrieve it, but Sally Connell was quick, lashing out with a vicious kick that caught Karen in the ribs, sending her sprawling. Within seconds, her hands closed round Karen's throat, squeezing with a strength born of pure, unadulterated hatred. Karen's vision blurred, dark spots dancing before her eyes as she struggled for air. But just as she felt herself slipping away, a series of gunshots rang out, and Sally's grip went slack. The woman slumped forward, a look of shock and disbelief etched on her face. Splatters of warm blood sprayed across Karen's face.

Karen pushed Sally Connell's limp body off her and staggered to her feet shocked and disorientated, gasping for air. Connell's lifeless eyes stared back at her, but the back of her head was missing with a gruesome bloodied mess of bone and glistening tissue remaining. The deadly headshot by one of the SAS soldiers had not only been lethal but within inches of Karen's face.

She stumbled over to Zac, and the two embraced, clinging to each other like lifelines amid the storm. The battle raged on. They had no time to take in the scene, before SAS soldiers clad in black with face protectors hauled them both to their feet and hurried them away from the firefight.

"Move, get a fucking move on," one screamed above the crescendo of noise that bounced off the stone walls.

Karen and Zac were frogmarched and unceremoniously pushed through a narrow passage towards another exit from the cave system. Approaching helicopters whipped up the air around them and drowned out further orders being barked at them by the soldiers that surrounded them in the darkened gloom, fast being lit up by their army transport.

A searing pain shot through her legs as her shins clattered on the metal lip of the helicopter side door. Karen landed flat on her face; the icy surface felt like a cold slap on her skin. The smell of jet fuel assaulted her nostrils as they hauled her inside, with Zac following seconds later as soldiers lifted his weak body in and closed the door behind them. With a roaring whir, the engine came to life as the cabin shook.

Karen lay numb to the outside world in the transport's rear clinging to Zac's broken body as the helicopter lifted off and disappeared into the dark of the night leaving Grozev's men to be cut down in a hail of rapid gunfire. She'd wanted Connell alive, but had she really? If faced with a face-to-face confrontation, Karen questioned whether she would have let Sally Connell live. A part of her wanted Connell to rot in jail, but a much bigger part wanted Connell dead, the ultimate payback for the misery and pain that wretched woman had caused Karen during her time in the Met.

39

NOT LONG AFTER a special forces helicopter whisked them away, they were transported to the hospital in a flurry of activity to face a long and exhausting night. Karen had never seen so many doctors and nurses fuss over them, with most of the attention being directed at Zac. He was semi-conscious and his condition concerned the doctors treating him. Dehydration, lack of food, little sleep, and beatings to his body had caused him to become a shadow of his former self.

Karen had waited outside while they treated him, and despite the best efforts of the medics to encourage her to be examined, she pushed away their concerns. Now Zac was with her again. She had no intention of losing sight of him.

The medical staff had moved Zac to a private room where they could closely monitor his condition. Karen spent the whole night beside his bed, holding his hand as he slept. They'd lightly sedated him, allowing his body to start the healing process. As she'd sat there she'd noticed the faint ligature marks round his neck. Karen had gritted her teeth in pure hatred and anger. She knew they hadn't wanted to kill him; it had been a game for Sally Connell. The woman had wanted to hurt Karen in as many ways as possible, and seeing her boyfriend threatened with a hanging was as barbaric as it got.

The first signs of light crept through the blinds. Her back was sore and stiff from sitting in the chair. But she wouldn't have it any other way. Despite pleas from the nurses to rest each time they came in to check on Zac, Karen refused to budge. She'd left his side twice to go to the loo, desperate to get back and keep her bedside vigil each time. The nurses had been amazing, coming in with cups of sugary tea and sweets to help her keep up her energy.

Karen yawned and let out a deep sigh. She was exhausted, the last dregs of adrenaline leaving her body hours ago. She glanced at Zac. He looked peaceful. What upset her the most was how thin and pale he looked. A few days of being held captive had left him with sunken cheeks and eyes. The extra weight he used to have round his chin was long gone, and his fingers seemed more bony than usual. She stroked the back of his hand. Dirt had gathered under his nails, and the tips of his fingers were grazed and bloodied. His wrist had a deep red and bruised line from the restraints, probably cable ties.

How could they have done this to him? Connell's plan was purely malevolent. She'd encountered individuals like her during her time in the force and professionally managed those situations. But this was too close to home because it affected her, which only made it more painful to accept.

A soft knock on the door tore her away from her thoughts. Chief Superintendent Kelly poked her head round the corner and gestured for Karen to join her outside. Karen slowly rose from her chair, her legs stiff, and sore. She made her way outside to meet Kelly in the corridor. The ACC and Captain Bird were there too.

"Ma'am, sir, captain," she said nodding at all three.

ACC Jackson nodded in reply. "We've already spoken to the doctors looking after Zac. The physical injuries will heal, none of them are life-threatening, as you know. His psychological recovery will be challenging."

"I know that, sir. I think anyone who has experienced what Zac has been through would be messed up."

"Of course. And how are you? Those final few moments were pretty intense."

Karen grimaced. She threw a glance in Captain Bird's direction before answering ACC Jackson's question. "Excuse my language, sir, but it was a fucking nightmare. I thought the SAS must have lost track of my location once we were in the cave."

Captain Bird folded his arms across his chest. "We hadn't lost your location at all. We weren't far behind you and needed to get all operators in place before we launched our rescue."

Karen glared at Bird. "Well, you took your bloody time," she snapped. Karen scrunched her eyes and pursed her lips. She hadn't meant to sound so aggressive. She held her hands up. "Sorry. So sorry. I didn't mean to have a go at you. Everything seemed to take so long to happen that it felt like it was ages before your boys came in."

Bird nodded. "Understandable. You were in a high-pressure situation. Time distortion is a bitch."

"Thank you. You cut it fine, bloody fine, but I can't tell you how relieved I was when it all kicked off. I can still hear the ringing in my ears now."

They all smiled, and Karen welcomed the light moment.

"How many were in there?" she asked.

"Fifteen hostiles."

"All dead?"

The captain nodded.

"Any casualties from your team?"

"Nothing other than a few cuts and bruises. It was a clean job. The boys did well."

Karen raised a brow. "As for the soldier who blew out Sally Connell's brains, I don't know whether to shake his hand or punch him in the face. He could have missed and taken me out as well."

Bird shook his head. "His laser sight planted the red dot slap bang in the middle of the back of her skull. He waited a few seconds for her to raise her head, so when the bullet passed through, it flew over the top of you. You weren't in danger."

Karen gave him a disbelieving stare, unsure whether to believe his *explanation*.

"Our officers have been in the cave system most of the night," ACC Jackson said. "They recovered a huge amount of evidence. A small arsenal of weapons, including semi-automatic rifles, a box of grenades, mobile phones, and more than a dozen radio sets. It was enough to supply a small army."

Kelly continued. "Officers discovered a shallow grave close by with the body of a white male. Shot through the head. He was missing an ear. Recently removed."

"I see. The hoax to make me think it was Zac's," Karen tutted.

"Yes." Kelly placed a hand on Karen's arm and gave it a gentle squeeze. "Some good has come out of this. You and the rest of our officers have all come back intact. With all the findings in the cave system, our hope is that the NCA and intelligence services will have enough evidence to shut down Grozev's OCG in the UK and Europe. We've sunk their immediate plans in the UK."

"Was the cave system their hideout?" Karen asked.

"No," Kelly replied. "The caving system comprised three separate caves all interconnected by narrow walkways. There were several entry and exit points. It made it easy for them to come and go... and escape if they needed to. The reason the SAS couldn't react straightaway was because they needed to position their soldiers to strike at all entry points simultaneously. By doing that, they could remove any possibility of getting away."

ACC Jackson cleared his throat. "Right, we'll let you get some rest. Of course we'll need to speak with both of you in the coming days."

Karen watched as they walked off in silence, disappearing through the double doors at the end of the corridor.

She returned to Zac's room. He was still asleep, but the hospital was waking. She could hear trolleys rattling along the corridors and a flurry of conversations as the nursing teams swapped over from the night shift to the day shift.

Karen had only taken a seat for a few minutes before there was another knock on the door. The FLO looking after Summer and Michelle appeared, but didn't enter, instead Summer rushed past her towards Karen with arms outstretched.

Karen jumped from her seat and swallowed Summer in a tight embrace. They both cried. Tears of happiness and comfort that lasted for a few minutes. Summer was in no hurry to let go, and neither was Karen. It was a moment she had longed for. And though her mind had been focused on bringing Zac home safely, Summer was never far from her thoughts. The love she had for this child was unbelievable and something she couldn't put into words. It was just a deep feeling, a sense of knowing how special this young girl was to her.

Summer turned and looked at her dad, her hand coming up to her mouth in shock. Tears followed straight away as she cried silently.

"Hey, come here," Karen said. She pulled Summer in for another hug.

"How is Dad?" Summer buried her face in Karen's hoodie, muffling her voice.

"He's good. He's a bit battered and bruised, but he's okay. Your Dad needs a lot of rest."

Summer looked up at Karen, her eyes red and swollen, tear stains streaking her cheeks. "Is it over?"

"Yes, darling. It is. *We* are all safe."

Karen glanced between Summer and Zac. They were her family, and she'd never been so relieved to see them. The entire ordeal had been terrifying, and as she stood there, she had no clue about how to rebuild their shattered lives. They had been through too much already.

But they would do it together. They had to.

"It's going to be okay, Summer. I promise."

40

Two days later.

With Zac resting, Karen visited Jade at home. Jade's parents had arrived in York and were staying with her. Her mother let Karen in and gave her a hug on seeing her. She told Karen that Jade was in her bedroom.

Karen peeked in to see Jade sitting up in bed, her phone in her hand as she scrolled through something.

"Budge up, make a bit of room for my fat lardy arse."

Jade stopped scrolling and looked up. She mustered a small smile as Karen came and sat on the bed beside her. Karen gave her a long hug and a kiss on the cheek. "How are you doing?"

Jade shrugged. "I go through good moments and then there are bad..."

Karen understood. She didn't need detailed explanations. She understood the effect that Jade's ordeal would cause for her. "I know. You must take it one day at a time. We all have to. Talking about it will help."

Jade shook her head. "I don't think I can. I don't know

where to begin. Thinking about it scares the living daylights out of me." Jade's eyes moistened as she sniffed.

Karen noticed the tremble in Jade's hands. "Listen, what you and Zac went through would shock anyone to the core. It's not something you can bury and forget about. That's the worst thing to do. Trust me, with the right help and enough time, you'll handle and process your experience in a way that helps you come to terms with what's happened. You might even come out stronger on the other side."

"I hope so, because at the moment, I can't imagine being a copper ever again."

Karen understood the sentiment. She had experienced that often during her career. After the ambush in London, and the death of a key witness and two officers in the convoy, Karen had been close to quitting the job. The fact that she was demoted from DCI to DI had shattered her. But with the help of occupational health and time to heal, she had found the strength to battle on and do the job she loved. In time, she hoped Jade would feel the same.

Karen tapped her on the arm. "Anyway, no need to think about that now. You need to rest, chill out, and let your mum and dad fuss over you."

Jade rolled her eyes. "I feel like I'm twelve years old again. Mum won't stop fussing over me. It's suffocating."

"She just cares. That's all. Listen, I'll let you rest."

"How are you holding up?" Jade asked.

Karen thought about it for a moment. "I don't know. I haven't had time to process anything. A part of me thinks it was a horrible dream. And then the reality of what we've been through hits me right between the eyes and knocks me for six."

"I'm glad Zac is all right. Give him my love when you

see him. We can organise a kind of weird survivor's party one day."

Karen furrowed her brow. "Is that such a thing?"

Jade pulled a face. "Dunno. It is now."

Karen left her to sleep.

THE STANDING OVATION and cheers weren't something Karen expected when she walked through the doors of the SCU. Despite pulling horrendous hours, her team was there at the forefront of welcoming her back.

Belinda was the first to rush up to her and give her a tight embrace as she burst out crying. Karen felt overwhelmed by the flood of emotions as she looked over Bel's shoulder to see a tearful Claire, Ed, Preet, Ned, and even Ty. At this rate they would need a man-sized box of tissues to mop up all the tears.

She spent the next few moments going round each of the desks giving everyone a hug before she gathered them at the front of the room. Karen asked them to quieten down as she had a few things to say. Once they were silent, Karen took a deep breath. It wasn't something she had planned to do, but it felt right.

"It's not often that I'm lost for words. And standing on the spot here, it's one of those rare moments. I can't thank each one of you enough for *everything* you've done. The long, unpaid hours..."

A few officers grumbled and teased Karen at that remark to wind her up.

"As I was saying, each and every one of you exceeded expectations and went above and beyond. You never gave up and you kept pushing. To say that I am in awe of my team and proud of you all, would be an understatement. I don't have words to describe what you've done for myself, Jade, and Zac. Jade and I came here as outsiders, and you took us under your wing, and you made us feel welcome." Karen's voice cracked. She cleared her throat, pushing back the tears that threatened to turn her into a blubbering mess.

"Despite everything that's happened in the last few days, moving to York was the best decision I've made in my career. I've had the privilege of working with amazing officers, and without moving to York, I wouldn't have met Zac."

"I bet Zac regrets that now!" someone shouted. The team erupted into a round of laughter.

"Ha, very funny, but you're probably right," Karen continued. "I'm not sure when Jade and I will be back to work, but soon. In the meantime, the super has agreed that Belinda and Ed will cover for us as joint acting SIOs, with the ongoing support of the super."

Belinda's jaw dropped as she looked at Karen and then to Ed, who looked equally surprised.

Karen turned to both of them. "Do me proud and don't fuck up."

Everyone laughed.

Karen thanked them again before leaving in search of DCI Shield. She found him knee-deep in paperwork, uttering something nonsensical to himself.

Karen tapped on his open door. He looked up, a surprised look on his face. He stood up and came round to the door.

"I wasn't expecting you in. You okay?"

"Getting there."

"And Zac?"

"Getting there as well but it will take longer."

Shield nodded. "Good. I'll pop over to the hospital in the next few days to say hello."

"He'd like that. I'm taking extended leave to sort out my head, but also to look after Zac. I need time away from this place."

An awkward silence hung between them.

Karen extended a hand. "I wanted to say thank you for everything you did for Zac and Jade. It meant a lot to me. I know we haven't seen eye to eye, but you handle things really well. I'm not sure I agree with your interviewing techniques," Karen said, referring to the prison visit, "but you get things done. Those are all things I can respect."

Shield hesitated for a moment before shaking Karen's hand.

"I don't suppose you do hugs, do you?" she asked. Karen leaned into him, arms outstretched.

Shield scrunched his nose and took a step back. "Nope. Hugs are for pussies. Now piss off and let me get on with my work."

Karen smiled. Shield would always be Shield. She stopped in his doorway and glanced over her shoulder to see Shield smiling back.

41

KAREN WAS BACK at Zac's bedside a few hours later. The euphoria of seeing her team had worn off, and now she felt so tired she struggled to keep her eyes open. The last few days seemed to have blurred into a confused and clouded memory that no matter how hard she tried to analyse, her subconscious mind wouldn't let her. It felt like it was protecting her from experiencing those awful feelings of desperation, fear, and sadness once again. Maybe she was trying too hard? Was it too soon? But she couldn't stop her mind from racing.

She looked at Zac. He had stirred a few times. What would happen to them? Would they ever be the same again? The thought crossed her mind whether they should start afresh somewhere else. Perhaps their experiences in York had left them with too many mental scars. But she couldn't keep running away. How could she ever find peace if she did that?

No. They had to be here. She knew the job came with risks. Okay, admittedly, what they had been through was rare and didn't sit in the category of acceptable risks. Life wasn't all plain sailing and picture-perfect. As she thought about it now, Zac, Summer, and herself, had all been through recent traumatic experiences. Maybe that was a good thing? A family of survivors.

That's what she wanted more than anything else. Family. Every day, she longed to come home to Zac and Summer. She wanted to enjoy family meals out, holidays, movie nights in on a Saturday night. And they had all of that. With a bit of time, patience, and the right help, they could get it back. She clung on to slivers of hope and wouldn't give up on that dream without a fight. She wouldn't let Sally Connell win. Connell paid... with her life. That chapter in her life was over.

A groan distracted her from her thoughts. She looked up to see Zac's eyes flicker. She jumped up from her seat and leaned into him.

"Hey, you. Missed you." She gave him a kiss on the forehead.

It took a few moments for Zac to come back into the room. His eyes danced round the ceiling before they settled on Karen. He tried to smile but winced.

"You're safe now. I'm so sorry. If it wasn't for me, you wouldn't be in this bed."

Zac shook his head and licked his dried, cracked, and bloodied lips. "Water."

Karen's eyes widened. "Shit, of course." She held the beaker with a flexi straw to his lips. He took a few sips before pulling away.

"This is none of your fault. It could have happened to anyone. It's just a bitch it happened to us. We'll get through this. You can't get rid of me that easily."

Karen's eyes welled up. She reached across and grabbed his hand, squeezing it. Waves of emotional happiness washed over her and stole her breath. She wanted to scream from the rooftops that she loved him.

"You sure? I won't blame you for walking away. Dating me should come with a Government health warning."

Zac tried to smile again. "We are in this together. I love you too much. Me and Summer both do."

Karen breathed a sigh of relief. It was all she wanted to hear. She stared at the man she loved. Yes, he looked like a sack of shit, and needed fattening up again, but Zac was her man, and that was how she always wanted it to be, through good times and bad.

She stared into his eyes, fighting back the tidal wave of emotions that threatened to leave her crumpled on the floor in a hysterical mess. She closed her eyes for a second as her mind spun. When she opened them, something deep inside told her it was the right thing.

Him. This. A family. Forever.

"Zac," she said, stroking the back of his hand, "will you marry me?"

Zac's eyes widened. They stared in silence for a moment, neither knowing what to say. Karen's cheeks flushed with embarrassment.

"Sorry? Say that again?" He whispered, his voice croaky and dry.

"Oh, God, I've embarrassed myself. But I mean it. I love you, Zac. And I love Summer like she's my own. I've never felt like this before with *anyone*, I want to spend the rest of my life with both of you. I want us to be a family. A proper family. Yes, we've got shit going on, and I don't know how we'll deal with what we've been through, but I know that together we'll be stronger. So, Zac, will you marry me?"

Zac stared at the ceiling for what felt like an eternity.

"Say something because at the moment I want to crawl under a rock and hide. I'm feeling a bit stupid."

"Well, it depends if you'll let me leave the toilet seat up, or not nag me when I don't do the beds in the morning or adjust the driver's seat in my car to suit you and not move it back, or...."

"Oi, you cheeky git. I'm being serious. If you don't answer, I'm withdrawing the offer!"

Zac rolled his eyes in mock resignation. "Okay, if I have to. Yes, I will marry you."

Karen smiled as she leaned in and kissed his lips. She stroked the side of his face and studied her man in silence. At that precise moment, and despite everything that had happened in the last few days, she had never felt happier.

As their laughter faded into the quiet comfort of the room, Karen's heart swelled with a joy she had thought she'd lost. She nestled closer, feeling the reassuring strength of Zac's presence. No, not just Zac now, her fiancé. The shadows of the recent past, once overwhelming and menacing, seemed to recede into mere echoes against the bright promise of their future together.

We survived, she thought, her eyes glistening with unshed tears. *Against all odds, we survived.* In Zac's smile, she saw not just the reflection of her love, but the dawn of a new start for them. She had no idea what they would do next, and despite a momentary flash of apprehension, she felt a sense of optimism that being part of family would take her life to a place she had only dreamt of.

"Forever," she whispered, a vow that filled the room with its quiet power. "Forever starts now."

JOIN MY READER'S GROUP

If you haven't already done so, then please join my reader's group for your free starter library, information about my writing, share in my journey as I research my next book, as well as news about my latest releases.

Join up to my VIP reader list here

CURRENT BOOK LIST

Hop over to my website for a current list of books:
http://jaynadal.com/current-books/

OTHER WAYS TO STAY IN TOUCH

Other ways you can connect with me:
Like my page on Facebook: Jay Nadal
Email jay@jaynadal.com with any questions, ideas or interesting story suggestions. Hey, even if you spot a typo that we've missed, then drop me a line!

ABOUT THE AUTHOR

Author of:
    The DI Scott Baker Crime Series
    The DI Karen Heath Crime Series
    The Thomas Cade PI Series

Printed in Great Britain
by Amazon